# The Case of the
# SCARY DIVORCE

## A Jackson Skye Mystery

by

# C. E. Pickhardt

illustrations by

# Jeff Fisher

C. E. Pickhardt
3311 Bryker Drive
Austin, Texas 78703
www.carlpickhardt.com
(512) 452-4543

Magination Press • Washington, DC

Library of Congress Cataloging-in-Publication Data

Pickhardt, Carl E.
    The case of the scary divorce: a Professor Jackson Skye mystery / by
C.E. Pickhardt.
        p.  cm.
    Summary: A ten-year-old boy meets the mysterious "Professor Jackson
Skye: Helping Investigator"who enlists his aid in solving eight cases, each
dealing with a problem he himself is experiencing during his parents'
divorce.
    ISBN 1-55798-457-3
    [1. Divorce—Fiction.  2. Afro-Americans—Fiction.]  I. Title.
PZ7.P552565Cas  1997
[Fic]—dc21                                                    96-44382
                                                                 CIP
                                                                  AC

Published by
MAGINATION PRESS
An Educational Publishing Foundation Book
American Psychological Association
750 First Street, NE
Washington, DC 20002

Manufactured in the United States of America
10 9 8 7 6 5 4 3 2 1

# TABLE OF CONTENTS

# CHAPTER ONE

## A Case of Forgetting

"**W**rite it down," you said, and so I have. Just keep in mind, it's been a while, and memory has ways of playing tricks, which is where I'll start, since that is where Professor Skye began with me. Professor who? Let me explain.

It was a long time ago. Now I'm fifteen. Back then I was only ten. Too young to keep up with everything that was going on, which was a lot. First Dad ran off with Marie. Then the divorce and moving to a cheaper place Mom could afford. Then me and my older sister in new schools we didn't like, living in a new neighborhood we didn't know. With so much to get used to, it was hard remembering all I should. And when I didn't, Mom got madder than she already was. She said she had enough to do without reminding me of what I had been told, much less tracking down what I had lost. She didn't care how important it was.

"Serves you right for keeping secrets!" My sister was enjoying my upset. Since the move, we had been fighting more than usual.

That was all right. I'd get her back later.

At the moment, I had a bigger problem. Where was the jar of money I had hidden from my sister and had forgotten how to find? Savings to buy Dad a Christmas present better than anything Marie could give. To convince him to come back home.

My sister and I had agreed to hate Marie. My sister even refused to visit Dad if she was there. So I did, too. Our plan was to be as mean toward her as we were nice to him. But without my money, I couldn't buy the gift. I felt like a pirate who had lost the map to his buried treasure. My sister had been right. Secrecy had done me in. No one could help me because I hadn't told anyone.

Frantic, I rummaged through the house and then the yard outside, looking anywhere and everywhere. No luck. Running back inside I ran into my mother, who wanted to know what was the matter. But I had already told her, and she hadn't listened.

"Nothing!" I moaned and continued dashing here and there, lifting up and looking underneath until, at last exhausted, I gave up and slumped down on the curb in front of our house.

I felt sorry for myself. I blamed myself. And I wished I had some company to understand my misery and help me out.

I sat for a long time and grew sadder and sadder, until I suddenly noticed that I was not alone. Seated beside me was a dark-skinned, gray-haired man gazing down at me through a pair of wire-rimmed glasses. His legs, even folded up, seemed extraordinarily long.

"It is unwise to lose things," he said. "Particularly things you value highly." His voice was like a hum, soft and deep, and he was smiling as he spoke.

"I didn't lose it on purpose, you know!" I snapped. Then I straightened up, staring in surprise.

"How did you know I lost something, and something special at that?" I eyed him suspiciously now, wondering if he had spied my money being hidden and taken it himself.

"Come, don't suspect me," he laughed. "I don't have it. But I can help you find it. If, indeed, you'd like some help. As for my knowing you had lost something of value, why, your actions told me that, upending anything not nailed down. Now, be quick, for I have other assistance to give. Will you be helped by a stranger or be helpless by yourself?" I considered his question. Although he spoke abruptly, he spoke kindly, so I decided to accept his offer.

"Yes," I agreed. "Yes, I would like some help." Then I told him what I had lost and said we should begin by looking in the house. But as I started to get up, he placed his hand upon my knee, pressing me back down.

"But I'm *sure* it's in the house," I insisted.

"It may well be," he replied, "but that is not the first place to investigate."

"Well, I just looked outside."

"You did. And it may well be there, too. But that is not the first place to investigate, either. Now describe to me again what you have lost."

"I told you! My jar of money is what I lost!" And I began to wonder if he could really help me after all.

"No," he disagreed. "No. That is not quite correct." He looked at me very intently, his voice dropping. "What has been misplaced is your *recollection* of where you hid the jar. A very different loss from the jar itself. A loss of memory."

"Then you're not going to help me find my savings after all," I complained. "Is that what you mean?"

Removing his glasses for a moment, he slowly rubbed the lenses with a corner of his jacket, then carefully put them back on.

"No, that is not what I am saying. You are not listening to my words, you are listening to your feelings. I will say it again. What you have lost is not the jar but the memory of where you hid it. So what I am going to do is help search your mind for the misplaced information. Far more efficient than rushing aimlessly about hoping to discover what you carelessly forgot. Your memory is out of order. I shall help you put it back. To begin, describe the jar to me."

"I told you! It's just a jar. A plain old jar."

"No jar is just 'a plain old jar.' Every jar is different. Among a hundred jars all made the same, each would in some small way remain unique. Try this: close your eyes and keep them closed until a picture of the jar comes clear. Then describe the image that appears."

I did as I was bid and was surprised that I could see the jar in more detail than when my eyes were open.

"It's a tall jar, about as tall as a pencil. The mouth is wide enough to fit my hand inside. The glass is clear. The top is red—plastic, I think. Smooth on the top, rough around the edges. And there's a patch of label shaped like a 'T' with the tail curled up. That's all. Except it smells like coffee." And I looked at him again.

The old gentleman was smiling.

"Much better. Now our search becomes precise. For a particular jar. Notice how memory plays tricks: keeping you from finding out what you know, and knowing more than you remember."

This was nonsense.

"How can a person know what they don't know and not know what they do? That's like saying I know where I hid my jar, when I don't."

He laughed. "Exactly! Don't expect the mind to be consistent just because it's in the business of making sense. You must only understand how it works. I shall help you. Memory is where we'll start."

I felt like he was going to teach me, and I didn't like the feeling because I didn't like school. So I said so.

"Yes, I am going to teach you. But not how you are taught in class. You will not be my student, but my apprentice. You will assist me in my work."

"You mean I'll have to work?" I hated work even more than school. "I don't want to work. Just help me find my money like you promised!"

"I'll keep my promise," he said. "Here, let me introduce myself." And from one of the many pockets in his faded green army jacket, he took out a small card.

Examining it, I read first one side:

> *Professor Jackson Skye,*
>
> *Helping Investigator.*

Then the other:

> *Problems solved*
>
> *upon request.*

"Is this you?" I asked.

He nodded, watching closely for my reaction.

"Professor?"

"Yes. Professor means 'qualified to teach.' I gave myself that title when I finally felt I had learned enough from hard experience to help other people."

I stared at the card a few moments, reluctant to let it go. I felt that returning it would mean not only that he had accepted my case, but that I had agreed to become his apprentice. At last, with a sigh, I gave it back.

"Good," he said as though an agreement had been struck. "Now let's begin. Since valued possessions are usually kept close at hand, we shall first consider your bedroom."

Once more I attempted to rise, but again he stopped me.

"Suppose," he asked looking back at the house, "I was standing in the doorway of your bedroom. What would I see?"

"Well," I thought for a moment, "against the far wall you'd see two beds—my sister's and mine. Then, to the left under the window, a toy chest. Then, to the right against the opposite wall, a bookcase and some shelves, a bureau and a closet—mostly my sister's stuff hanging in there, with my stuff piled on the floor." I paused to check for anything important I had missed.

"This will serve as a beginning," he remarked. Then he added thoughtfully, "Sharing a room would make it hard to conceal something from each other."

I agreed.

"There isn't any place, which makes my sister furious. I've found her diary each time she's hidden it. Once in the lower drawer beneath her underwear. Once under the mattress. I could feel the lump. And last week in the pinned-up leg of her blue jeans hanging in the closet."

"This is beside the point, I know, but why don't you leave your sister's things alone?"

I looked at Professor Skye in surprise. How could anybody supposed to be smart ask such a foolish question?

"Because getting her angry is the best way to get her back when she's been teasing me, or even when she hasn't."

"I should have known," he sighed. "Well, one lesson at a time." Then something seemed to catch his attention. "Was your sister angry when you found her diary again?"

7

"Was she ever!" I smiled as I remembered. "We really got into it!"

"Tell me," said Professor Skye softly, "everything you can recall about the fight. It may give us a clue."

"All right. But I don't think the fight will show us where to look."

"Maybe not. But tell me anyway."

"Well, she was gossiping with her new friend, Janet, which is why I never get to use the phone, because they're always on it. So, to get her back, I got her diary. When she came into our room, I was sitting on the bed reading all that stupid stuff about boys. She got really mad. She grabbed it from me, saying what a brat I was, and I said she was a brat for hogging the phone. I said I'd find her diary wherever she hid it. And she said, 'Oh yeah?'—well, she could get me back anytime she wanted because she knew where my money jar was hidden.

"And she did know, because she reached into the bottom of the toy chest and pulled it out. I jumped up to grab it. I pushed her and she pushed me, and I hit her and she punched me. And just as I was going to kick her a good one, the jar fell to the floor and smashed to bits! Money scattered everywhere! What a mess! Then, on account of being barefoot, she cut her heel on the glass and started crying, screaming it was all my fault, which it wasn't. So I screamed back, hadn't she ever heard of wearing shoes?

"Then Mom came in, screaming at both of us to stop screaming, and wouldn't listen to either of us tell our side. She sent my sister off to fix her foot and ordered me to begin sweeping up, no argument, did I understand? Because she wasn't interested in who started the fight, only in getting it stopped. Which wasn't fair, leaving me to do the cleaning up while my sister pretended to be hurt.

"Then Mom made her come back to help, but I said, 'No,' I'd do it myself. It was my jar. Besides, my sister would only steal the money, because she was a thief. And she called me a 'busybody' for always nosing into things that weren't my business. And we would have gotten into it again, except Mom gave both of us that look that meant she'd had enough, so we backed off.

"Mom handed me a new jar and told my sister to let me do it. She told me to call when I was done, so she could check I hadn't missed any broken glass. So when I was left alone, I gathered up the money and put it in the new jar, peeling off most of the label. Then I called my sister to come help with all the glass, but she refused because I'd said I didn't want any help, which Mom said was okay. I said, 'You wait till I find your diary again.' And she yelled back, 'Well, wait till I find your money jar again!' And I yelled back she'd have to find it first. I lifted up the windowsill, which was loose, and dropped the jar between the walls just before Mom stomped in, yelling at us both to stop yelling and settle down, because the next one who picked a fight with the other was going to have a fight with her, did we understand? We did.

"And that's all I remember, except, later that night on the phone to Janet, her new friend, my sister said I was a 'pesky brat,' but I said I wasn't, from the extension where I'd been listening the whole time. And she told Mom, who told me to get off the phone and leave my sister alone, like she always does, playing favorites, taking my sister's side. So I went back into the bedroom looking for my sister's diary, but I couldn't find it."

"I see," said Professor Skye, giving me a quizzical look, as if I was a hard puzzle for him to solve. "Well, at least we've learned where your money jar is, if nothing else."

"We have?" I asked, wondering where.

"Beneath the windowsill, you said. Stuffed between the walls."

Had I said that? I had said that! All Professor Skye had done was listen.

"You're right!" I exclaimed. "I knew it all the time. I just forgot!"

And I jumped up and rushed into the house to make sure my savings were still there. I ran into the bedroom, over to the window, and lifted up the sill. There was my jar, just where I had stashed it. Safe and sound!

Well, you can imagine how excited I was, feeling good again. I ran back out to tell the news to Professor Skye, because although I was the one who had remembered, he *had* tried to help. But he was nowhere to be seen. I looked up one end of the street and down the other. I even called his name several times. No Professor Skye. Had my imagination been playing tricks? Like my memory? He appeared and disappeared so quickly. I began to wonder if he had been real. Until I noticed writing in the dust.

A message: "See you then, Prof. Skye."

There, I hadn't made him up! But when was 'then'? And where? And how was I supposed to know? I wasn't. Oh well, at least he helped me find my money.

What a relief! Now I could buy Dad a present. But what? What would be good enough to bring him back? At supper I was quiet, thinking hard. Later, as I lay in bed, questions kept me awake. That's why I dreaded night. My fears and worries came out in the dark. What if Dad didn't come back? What if he stayed with Marie? Even worse, what if they got married? My answers were more scary than my questions. I thought I'd never get to sleep. But at last I did.

# CHAPTER TWO

## A Case of Fear

Bad news came with Dad's monthly check: he and Marie were getting married.

Mom cried pretty hard when she told us. We tried to comfort her, not really knowing what to say. Except my sister promised she'd never love Marie, only Mom.

"Now what?" was all I could think. No more dreaming of Mom and Dad getting back together. No more seeing Dad without Marie.

I thought divorce was scary, but this was worse. I wished I could get angry like my sister, instead of feeling worried. After she fell asleep at night, I lay awake asking, "What if?" What if Mom got so tired and unhappy she couldn't care for us? Where would we go? Not to Dad's. Not if Marie hated us the way we hated her.

What if Dad chose Marie instead of us, like he had chosen her instead of Mom? If he could stop loving Mom, maybe he could stop loving us. What if my sister and I were left alone, with no one to take care of us? Or we were sent to live with strangers? Bedtime was for worrying.

Too bad Professor Skye wasn't around to help. Professor Skye. Did he mean what he had said? That I would be his apprentice? Probably not. But I wished he had. I never even got to thank him for helping find my money.

Of course, I told my mom and sister about Professor Skye, but they thought this was more of my pretending. More of my stories. Just because I liked to make things up, Mom sometimes found it hard to believe me. Oh, I'd tell the truth all right, but then I'd add some make-believe to make the truth even better. If I took extra long before getting something done, it was because the clocks got tired and slowed down to take a rest. "Tell me another story that's a little closer to the truth," Mom would say. "One that I won't have such a hard time believing." So I'd take out some of the make-believe, even though the story was never near as good. But not this time. Professor Skye had been real!

"Oh sure, listen to Mr. Maker Upper!" teased my sister.

"You're getting too old to be telling stories," warned my mom.

"It's not a story. It's the truth!" I yelled. I wished I had invited Professor Skye into the house to see the jar and meet my mom and sister. But it was too late now. I had no idea how to find him.

So I decided to forget Professor Skye. But I couldn't. The harder I tried not to think about him, the more I couldn't think of anything else. Professor Skye had been right. I did need to get my memory in order. First I had forgotten what I wanted to remember, and now I was remembering what I wanted to forget. Not the only thing that was going wrong.

For two days in a row I had forgotten to turn in all my homework, so Mom had agreed with the teacher that I should be kept after to make it up. This made me stay later than usual, which Mom hoped would teach me a lesson. She knew I didn't want to spend any more time at school than I had to already.

So, for no particular reason, I thought then, I detoured through the park on my way home and stopped by the big slide. Leaning back against it, I made roads in the sand with the toe of my shoe.

"Look out below!" called a familiar voice. Glancing up, I saw Professor Skye slipping down the slide. In the late afternoon light, his hair appeared more silver than gray, and his glasses reflected the sun into my eyes. He still wore his faded green army jacket. And seeing his legs stretched out before him reminded me how tall he was.

"I'm glad you were prompt in keeping our appointment," he announced.

"Our appointment?" I asked.

He waved my question away with his hand. Then, catching my confusion, he waved it back again.

"Last time we met, I arranged this meeting time without telling you. That you understood our arrangement without my putting it in words is indicated by your being where I said and when."

"This is just a coincidence," I protested. "I didn't come here on purpose. This is an accident."

"You can believe that if you choose," replied Professor Skye, lowering his voice, which I later figured out he did when he had something important to say. "But I do not. People can believe in accidents to avoid responsibility. To be in the wrong place at the wrong time is a person's choice. So is being in the right place at the right time. Which is your choice today. So I do not call this accidental. Besides, why would I be here to meet you if I wasn't sure you were going to meet me? A waste of time.

"Now, we have only a few minutes before our appointment arrives. Tell me about your family not believing what you said about me."

I looked at him sharply. "Were you watching the whole time?"

"I do not need to see you to know about you," he said. "It's natural that you would tell your family about me, that they would not believe you, and that you would feel betrayed by their response."

"Well, you're right," I answered. "I did tell my mom and sister about you. And they didn't believe me!"

"It sounds improbable even to me. You happen to meet a strange old man on the street who, without even looking for it, helps you recover a lost object! No, if I were your family, I'd have a hard time believing such a tale. Wouldn't you?"

"No!" I disagreed. "I would not. Parents are supposed to believe their children. To trust them. Maybe not the things children make up, but when they tell the truth. Mom should have believed me, and she didn't. That's not right!"

"It's not?" asked Professor Skye. "Do you believe everything she tells you?"

"When she tells me the truth, I do," I retorted.

"And when she doesn't?"

"Then I don't believe her," I answered, getting irritated at the ever-tightening circle of thinking he was winding me up in.

Although Professor Skye spoke softly and was gentle in his manner, nothing could stop him when he had something to teach.

"How do you *know* when she is telling the truth and when she's not?" he asked.

"Well, I just have to decide, that's all."

"On what basis do you make that decision?" he persisted.

The conversation was getting tiresome, and I felt like going home.

"It's getting dark," I observed, glancing around. "I wonder what time it is."

"It's time to talk about truth," said Professor Skye, ignoring what he knew my question meant. "Our appointment should be here any moment."

Who? I wanted to ask, but didn't.

"In our work," he began, "there is always a problem with truth. Like the gentleman today. What, about what he will be describing, is the truth and what is not? Our help depends upon the answer. He brings a problem. Like losing your money jar, only more serious. Because his problem frightens him. And fear can be a very serious problem. Who's afraid of the Big Bad Wolf? We all are. But the Wolf is different for everyone."

I didn't like the familiar sound of the problem, and was about to excuse myself when Professor Skye looked over my shoulder.

"Ah," he said, "here he comes now."

And I turned around to look.

Approaching us across the playground was a boy who appeared a year or so younger than me. He had blond hair and was kind of plump. His hands were in his pockets, his head was bowed down, and his shoulders hunched over.

"Hello, Mr. Sonny McWalter!" greeted Professor Skye merrily.

"Hello, Professor Skye," mumbled the new boy, looking at me suspiciously.

"Mr. McWalter, meet Mr. Wallaby Bump," responded Professor Skye, indicating me by that name with a nod in my direction. Of course, this was not my name. At least not until then. But I just greeted Sonny McWalter as though it was. I figured Professor Skye wanted to call me that for reasons of his own, which, like a lot about him, was hard to understand.

"Mr. Bump," continued Professor Skye, "is my assistant. He is very helpful to me and will not repeat to anyone what we discuss." And here he gazed directly at me, securing my assent.

Then, standing up, he led Sonny McWalter over to the swings, indicating with a look behind that I should follow, which I did. Soon each of us was seated on a swing, Sonny McWalter between Professor Skye and me.

"Now, Mr. McWalter," began Professor Skye. "To refresh my memory and to introduce your difficulty to Mr. Bump here, could you go back over what you were telling me the other day?"

Sonny McWalter was silent for a while, swinging slightly back and forth, summoning up his will to talk when he clearly di ' not want to. At last he turned to me and spoke.

"Have you ever been afraid?" he asked, sounding sad and weary. "Have you ever been afraid of the dark?"

I nodded, without mentioning my own worrying at night.

"I am afraid of the dark," he admitted. "In bed, I am afraid to close my eyes because the monster might get me."

"The monster?" I asked. The question just popped out.

"Yes. It hides in the shadows, so it's hard to see. Staring back is how I back it off. But it won't leave. It just watches me. Then, when I look away, it inches closer."

"Has the monster been with you long?" I asked.

"I don't know," he replied. "I only noticed it three months ago. Maybe it was there all the time, waiting for me. At first it came out once or twice a week after we moved here for Dad to make a fresh start. But soon it was there every night, creeping out from the darkest corner of my room. At the same time each night. Right after I'm in bed and my lights have been turned out."

I listened and said nothing, hoping Professor Skye would speak. But he did not. Nobody talked. The silence grew uncomfortable. Somebody needed to say something. So I saved the conversation by offering a solution.

"Why don't you keep your lights on? That way there won't be any dark for the monster to hide in."

But he shook his head.

"I tried, but my mother said I'd wake up exhausted sleeping with the lights on. And my father got angry, because we have enough money problems right now without wasting electricity on something foolish."

"Do you sleep at all?" I asked, wondering if monster watching kept him up all night.

"Very carefully," he answered. "On and off. For short periods. Waking up to make sure the monster keeps its distance. If it has crept too close, I force it back into the corner. I shine my flashlight in its eyes."

It was then I noticed that Sonny McWalter had a flashlight clipped to his belt.

"How come you carry that with you?" I asked. "I thought the monster just lived in your room."

Sonny McWalter glanced nervously about.

"At first it did. But just like you said it would"—and here he looked at Professor Skye—"the monster has begun following me around to other places now. Which is when you said to come back and see you. So I have. I'm afraid it has followed me here tonight."

"I hope so," said Professor Skye sincerely. "I have wanted to meet your monster. Monsters have always been of interest to me. Over the years I have met up with a number of them."

Well, I had heard enough of this nonsense. I was about to interrupt and say, didn't Professor Skye know monsters weren't real and only lived in people's imaginations, when he silenced me with a warning glance. He went on talking with Sonny McWalter.

"Of course, each monster is different from every other—each frightening in its own way. Perhaps, while we wait for it to grow darker and for the monster to show itself, you can describe yours to me."

Sonny McWalter drew into himself, like he was taking a deep breath of courage, and slipped the flashlight off his belt into his hand. His voice was quavering now.

"Professor Skye, what's going to happen? What do you suppose it's going to do? What shall I do?"

"What will happen," reassured Professor Skye, "is that the monster will appear. Then you and I will go and meet the monster. After that you won't be troubled anymore."

"But when we meet the monster, Professor Skye, after we meet it, what are you going to do?" asked Sonny McWalter. "Are you going to fight it or frighten it or what?"

Professor Skye placed his hand on Sonny McWalter's shoulder, quieting the shuddering and steadying the fear.

"Sometimes it is possible to fight a monster, but the harder you fight, the harder it fights back. So when the fight is over, the monster has grown stronger than before. So we are not going to fight the monster. As for frightening it away, as you do with your flashlight, you have seen how the creature soon returns. So we will not try to scare it off. Instead, we are going to gentle the monster. We are going to tame it. I will show you how to do this, but I cannot do it for you. To tame the monster, you will have to brave your fear. Now, tell me in detail what your monster looks like."

Sonny McWalter cleared his throat, then haltingly began to do as Professor Skye had bid.

"It is very large. Hunched over. With pointed ears and glowing eyes. It crouches and it shuffles and it sways from side to side. I can hear its breathing like the roaring of a fire." And Sonny McWalter grew very quiet as the darkness settled about us.

"Thank you," said Professor Skye. "This is very helpful. I begin to see the kind of monster you are up against."

Then, so quickly it caught me by surprise, Sonny McWalter swiveled in his seat and beamed his flashlight toward an overhanging tree a little way behind us, under which were some thick bushes. Despite his body shaking, he held the flashlight very steady.

"So it has arrived," Professor Skye announced. "Good." And he stood up and faced the bushes behind us. "Now, Sonny McWalter, come and stand beside me and give me your hand."

Moving very carefully, Sonny McWalter obeyed. As he did so, he shifted the flashlight to his other hand, while keeping the beam where it was pointed.

"What we are about to do, Sonny McWalter," continued Professor Skye, "we must do in the dark."

"No!" protested Sonny McWalter. "I can't!"

"Yes," insisted Professor Skye. "Yes, you can. I want you to shut off the flashlight and give it to Mr. Wallaby Bump."

"But I'm afraid!" protested Sonny McWalter.

"Of course you are afraid," agreed Professor Skye. "Who wouldn't be afraid when a monster was pursuing them? But do you want to keep on being afraid?"

"No," murmured Sonny McWalter. "No, I don't."

"Then," explained Professor Skye, "here is what we must do. Instead of letting the monster stalk us, we are going to stalk the

19

monster. It is less frightening to be the hunter than the hunted. And it feels safer not to hunt alone. I shall be with you, by your side, to encourage and guide, if you will let me. But first, you must give up the light."

Well, Sonny McWalter hesitated a long time before finally handing me the flashlight, still shining toward the bushes.

Now you must understand, I didn't see any monster and would have said so. I would have gone over to the bushes to prove there wasn't any monster, if Professor Skye had let me. But he didn't. This was not his plan. In fact, his plan seemed just the opposite. He was treating make-believe like it was real. He was acting like there was a monster, when I knew there wasn't. But what could I do but go along with his pretense, if that was what he wanted? So I did what he asked.

"Turn off the flashlight, Mr. Bump," Professor Skye instructed. I turned it off and saw Sonny McWalter step over tight beside Professor Skye.

"Come on, Sonny McWalter," encouraged Professor Skye. "Let's begin. As we creep forward, I want you to look very carefully for the monster, and as soon as you see it, squeeze my hand."

I heard no reply from Sonny McWalter, but he must have agreed, because I saw the tall, thin shape of Professor Skye and that of his much shorter companion begin to move forward, slowly advancing toward the bushes. Suddenly they stopped. Sonny McWalter let out a cry of alarm.

"How close is it?" I heard Professor Skye whisper.

"It's coming out, Professor Skye! It's coming to get us!"

"Ah, yes," said Professor Skye softly. "I see it now. Let's try to move around behind it. Tell me if it follows us."

And, more quickly now, they circled to their right until their backs were to the bushes and they were facing me.

"It's right in front of us!" wailed Sonny McWalter. "Look out! It's right between us and Wallaby Bump!"

"So it is," replied Professor Skye (although I didn't see anything but darkness between us), "and now we have it, Sonny McWalter. We have it trapped!"

"We—we do?" stammered Sonny McWalter.

"Yes, we do," affirmed Professor Skye. "And here we go! Hold tightly to my hand and stretch as wide apart as you can reach."

In the dark I saw them separate but remain connected.

"Now, Sonny McWalter, this is the moment. Will you do exactly as I ask?"

I couldn't hear the reply to Professor Skye's question.

"Bump!" he called sharply to me. "Shine the light over here!"

I did, and Sonny McWalter let out a shriek of surprise, cut short by Professor Skye's command:

"Grab my other hand!"

I don't know who grabbed who, but their free hands joined together surrounding what their encircled arms enclosed.

"We have it, Sonny McWalter! It has been driven by the light into our trap!"

But Sonny McWalter only seemed to be straining to escape the old man's grasp, which would not let him go.

"Sonny McWalter, Sonny McWalter," called Professor Skye. "Stop pulling away. Stop and look at what your courage has caught. Open your eyes!" At this command, the struggling ceased. "Open your eyes. You have hunted what was hunting you. You have captured what you feared."

Although I couldn't see clearly, Sonny McWalter must have opened his eyes because I heard him whisper to Professor Skye: "Oh, it's so close. I can feel it up against me. How can it be so close and not hurt me? How can it crouch so small to fit between us?"

Professor Skye was silent for a while before replying. "Monsters usually grow smaller after you have caught them. And in captivity they become less hurtful."

"And less frightening," added Sonny McWalter, his voice filling with wonder.

"And less frightening," Professor Skye agreed.

"Even the breathing. Not a roaring at all. More like a gentle blowing. Can you feel it?"

"Yes," said Professor Skye. "Even the sound can change."

"What do we do with it now?" asked Sonny McWalter.

"We tame it," came the answer.

"How? Tell me how!" Sonny McWalter wanted to know.

"You tame a monster by doing just what you are doing now. You tame a monster by getting to know it. By getting close to it and letting it get close to you. By following your fear toward what you fear. By hunting it instead of letting it hunt you. By doing exactly what you have done. By being brave. You tame a monster in all these ways and one way more: you call the monster by a name."

"But I don't know its name," confessed Sonny McWalter.

"Then you should give it one," suggested Professor Skye. "For the name it has is the name you give it."

"Well," considered Sonny McWalter, "before I would have given it a ferocious name, but now I think I won't. I'd rather call it something friendly."

"That sounds like a good idea," said Professor Skye.

"What about 'Mr. Good Night'?" asked Sonny McWalter.

"Why don't you ask the monster? Offer the name and see if it accepts."

And that must have been what Sonny McWalter did. And the name must have been accepted, because he released his hold on Professor Skye and dropped his hands to his sides, breaking the trap like a broken spell.

"Well done!" congratulated Professor Skye. "The last way to tame a monster, the way I could not tell you, and you have done it. The final way to tame a monster is to let it go."

"But see," exclaimed Sonny McWalter, " how it doesn't run away. How it stays close. I think it likes me!"

"I think it does," agreed Professor Skye. "I think it does. Perhaps it would enjoy keeping you company awhile. As long as you'd enjoy keeping company with it."

"Do you think it would come home with me?" asked Sonny McWalter.

"Why don't you walk in that direction and see if it will follow?"

And that is just what Sonny McWalter did. He walked slowly away from Professor Skye, past me, across the darkened playground toward the lighted street beyond, occasionally looking back over his shoulder to make sure his friend was keeping up with him.

Puzzled by what had happened, I watched him depart until I felt Professor Skye watching me.

"The question you want to ask," he said, "is this: Did the monster truly exist?"

"Well, did it?" I was disturbed by how easily he could break into my thoughts.

"I will answer your question by asking you another," Professor Skye said. "Do you believe Sonny McWalter was truly afraid?"

I thought for a moment.

"Yes. Yes, I do."

"Then," concluded Professor Skye, "for all practical purposes, the cause of his fear, the monster, did exist. Truth is simply what a person chooses to believe is true. Accepting the truth of another person's belief doesn't mean you have to believe it yourself. Like this afternoon. You didn't believe in Sonny McWalter's monster for yourself, but you believed in it for him. And because you did, you helped him change what he feared into what he liked. Monsters can be blessings in disguise. Although I don't know how grateful Sonny McWalter will feel when he discovers you have not returned his flashlight."

Professor Skye was right! I hadn't noticed. Immediately I sprinted after Sonny McWalter, catching up to him just as he reached the street. He took the flashlight and thanked me for remembering.

Out of breath from my sudden run, I turned back to the swings, but Professor Skye was nowhere to be seen. Like the last time, he had appeared and disappeared when I did not expect it. Oh well, perhaps I'd see him at our next appointment, if we'd made one.

Walking home, I wondered what Professor Skye had meant for me to learn. The only monster I could think of in my life was Marie. I hoped she wasn't going to be as awful as I feared. Pretty soon, when they got back from their honeymoon, I'd have to see her on my visit. Maybe she wouldn't be so bad after all. Who knows, we might even become friends.

"Boy, are you in trouble now!"

23

It was my sister, glad to see me getting home so late. And I would have been in for it, except she got in trouble first. Watching out for me, she had forgotten to watch the stove like she'd been told, and supper boiled over and she had to clean it up. What a mess! Maybe things were starting to look up.

At least, when it was time for bed, I didn't lie awake and worry. I slept the whole night through.

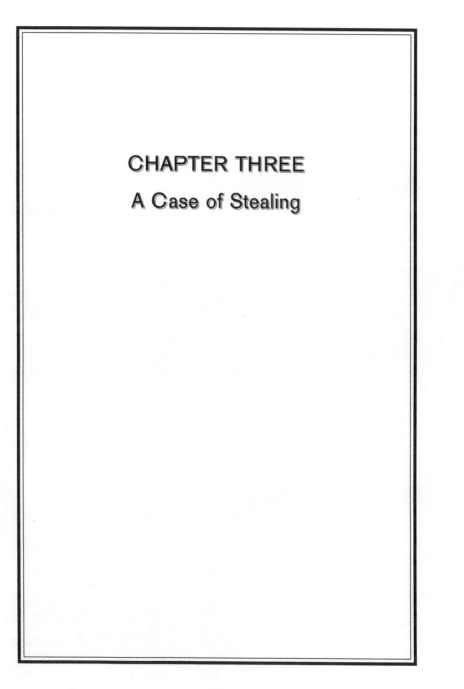

# CHAPTER THREE

## A Case of Stealing

That was the trouble with Saturdays: straightening the house. Me and my sister were put to work until Mom was satisfied that everything was neat and clean. Of course, I got the hardest jobs, the heavy stuff, because I was a boy. No use complaining. My mom would always make the same excuse.

"Now you're the man of the house, that's why."

It wasn't fair, and she knew it. Favoring my sister. Being harder on me just showed who she loved best. My sister. Because they were both girls.

Only one good thing about being a boy: I got some freedom that my sister didn't. What Mom refused my sister because it wasn't safe, she let me do to make me independent. So when all my chores were done, on Saturdays I was allowed to walk down to Lakeland Mall, wander among the weekend crowd, and stare into store windows. With a dollar in my pocket and a promise to be home no later that 3:00 in the afternoon, Mom would let me go.

My favorite store was Bolster's. On Saturdays it was always filled with shoppers, like a big party of people having fun buying what they wanted.

My first stop on entering Bolster's was the snack counter for a bag of hot, fresh popcorn. With the warmth of the bag tucked under my arm and the good salty taste of the popcorn in mouth, I rode the escalators. I loved to ride the escalators! Passing floor after floor. Watching people coming down as I went up, and watching them come up as I came down, I created stories in my mind about whoever caught my fancy.

I had just storied a little pointy-faced man clutching a box into a spy stealing secrets, when suddenly I saw Professor Skye on the opposite escalator riding up. I opened my mouth to call out a greeting when he shook his head to stop me. He whispered as we passed:

"Not now! See you there." And we were parted before I could reply.

See me where? I wondered, then shrugged the question off. There was no point in asking when no answer could be given. Apparently, I had caught Professor Skye in the middle of some investigation, and he did not want me to interfere. So I continued my ride and put him out of my mind.

I got off the escalator at the third floor to buy a cold drink at the cafeteria. The salty popcorn had made me thirsty. Thank goodness, the line at the counter was short. I was reaching into my pocket for my money when I heard a familiar voice calling my name. Looking around, I saw Professor Skye seated in the booth behind me, peppering a fried egg. He indicated with his other hand that I should take the seat across from him, at which was placed a tall glass of cola.

I sat down and waited for Professor Skye to speak, but he simply nodded toward the soda and continued peppering his egg until it was thoroughly blackened.

"This is an example," he finally declared, following my stare to his plate, "of how imitation can lead to excess. When I was your age, I admired my father a great deal and wanted to be like him in every way. Among his distinguishing habits was peppering his food beyond recognition. Determined to be similar, I began peppering my food, despite the burning that it caused my mouth. Over many years, what I began in order to copy my father, I continued in order to please the taste I had developed. So you see me as I am now: somewhat wise from all my years and somewhat foolish in my habits. But here is something worth remembering: Who we are and how we are have a lot do with whom we choose to copy."

"Is that why you still eat so much pepper?" I asked. "To be like your father?"

"No," he laughed. "In the beginning was the desire to imitate. In the end was the habit. A great motivator, imitation. It causes us to do a thing simply because we admire others who are doing it. Perhaps in the hope that if we are like them, they will like us. But imitation can be a trap, leading someone like myself into bad habits. Or even into serious mistakes. Which is the case we have in hand today. But you can form your own opinion when they arrive. Now, I want to thank you for not greeting me on the escalator."

"I wanted to," I replied. "I was going to."

"Yes," he grew serious and his voice dropped. "But you honored my request, even though you did not know the reason for it. This required trust. Very important, this thing called trust. Without it, people can suspect each other's intentions, question their caring, disbelieve what they are told, even fear the other is conspiring to do them harm. Trust is very strong and very fragile. And, once broken, it can take a long time to rebuild. How to recover trust after it has been lost: this is the problem we are going to have to help today. This matter between Regina Lee and her mother."

This was now the second time Professor Skye had mentioned the help we would be giving, but I was getting better at waiting, so I did not ask for more than I was told. Maybe he was trying to teach me patience.

Instead I asked a different question: "Are you saying everybody should trust everybody, then?"

"No. No, that is not what I am saying. While distrust and loss of trust create great difficulties between people, misplaced trust can lead to danger."

"I trust you, Professor Skye," I said.

"I know you do," he nodded. "You trusted me when you accepted my offer of help, and you took a chance when you did. I might have advised you badly. Or used what I learned to take advantage of you. The power to help is always the power to hurt. Help is risky to receive, which is why both mother and daughter want help from us and don't want help from us at the same time. As you shall see." And Professor Skye stopped speaking and looked away.

I turned to follow his gaze, seeing as I did so a tall, light brown-skinned woman enter the snack bar, pause a moment to survey the booths, and fix her eyes on Professor Skye. Her lips pursed tight, she strode over to where we were sitting, stopping so abruptly that all the bracelets on her wrists and strands of beads around her neck jangled to announce her arrival. She glared down at Professor Skye.

29

"I am Regina Lee's mother!"

"And this," replied Professor Skye nodding toward me, "is my assistant, Mr. Tall Walker. Won't you sit down."

I shrunk back into the corner of the booth as the angry lady sat herself beside me. I wanted to introduce myself properly by my real name instead of this foolish-sounding one Professor Skye saw fit to give me, but I felt correcting his introduction would only make things worse.

"You might have picked a more private place to meet!" snapped Regina Lee's mother at Professor Skye.

"I might have," he amiably agreed. "But the advantage of working out differences in a public place is that people are more likely to keep their voices down and their emotions under control. Fear of attracting public notice acts as a restraint."

Then he leaned back and looked directly at me as though expecting I should continue the conversation. I looked back at him. Regina Lee's mother looked down at me. Both of them were now looking at me, and I was more uncomfortable than ever.

"Why do you look at the boy?" broke in Regina Lee's mother. "He has no business in this, no business being here at all!"

But Professor Skye remained silent, looking at me as if I was supposed to say something, so in desperation I finally did.

"Is your daughter going to join us soon?" I asked, hoping this would relieve the tension.

"Child, I don't know who you are or why you are here. I don't know if my daughter will join us. And I don't know why *he* had my daughter deliver me this note from him last evening." She slapped down on the table a small white envelope, as though confronting Professor Skye with evidence of some wrongdoing.

I started at the sudden sharpness of the noise, but Professor Skye seemed undisturbed, although he was watching Regina Lee's mother closely.

"I don't know what's going on here!" I blurted out, upset to be caught in so much awkwardness and anger. "Professor Skye, what is this all about?"

"It's about this," softly replied Regina Lee's mother, "it's about this, Child." And she opened the envelope, withdrawing and unfolding a small sheet of yellow paper which bore the following hand-printed message:

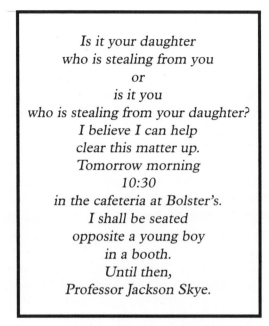

*Is it your daughter
who is stealing from you
or
is it you
who is stealing from your daughter?
I believe I can help
clear this matter up.
Tomorrow morning
10:30
in the cafeteria at Bolster's.
I shall be seated
opposite a young boy
in a booth.
Until then,
Professor Jackson Skye.*

"This is your note?" she asked Professor Skye. The anger had gone out of her voice and she seemed only sad and perplexed.

"Yes," replied Professor Skye.

"Do you really believe your daughter is a thief?" I asked, feeling braver now that Regina Lee's mother had softened toward me.

"I don't know what to believe, Child. For sure, these last two months, money has been disappearing from my purse, and Regina Lee has new jewelry to wear she has no business buying on the small allowance she gets. But when I ask her how she bought a bracelet or a ring or a necklace, she answers she can spend her money any way she wants. And when I ask about the money, she gets angry and goes on and on about how I'm so much harder on her than on the other children and how it hurts that I don't trust her. Then she ends in tears and so do I. That's why I'm here."

"You are," repeated Professor Skye. "As is Regina Lee."

And coming our way, hesitant, eyes examining the floor, slowly approached a very dark-skinned girl of about my age, but much taller than me.

"Hello, Regina Lee," smiled Professor Skye, moving over so she could sit beside him.

"Hello, Professor Skye. Hello, Mama. Hello," she nodded at me. I nodded back. Like her mother, she wore a lot of jewelry, but her skin was so much darker than her mother's that at first I didn't notice their physical resemblance—the large intense eyes and the strong square jaw. It occurred to me that in a battle of wills, neither was likely to come out the winner.

"I see you're wearing a new ring," observed Regina Lee's mother accusingly. "You got it from upstairs, because I saw it there. I even tried it on. Six dollars. Girl, where did you get that kind of money? If you won't tell me, then tell your friend Professor Skye here!" And now she turned on Professor Skye. "You arranged this meeting. Why don't you make her tell the truth, and we'll get this cleared up once and for all!"

"It's my money, Mama," retorted Regina Lee with equal fury. "You're always blaming me!"

Then both looked away from each other to ease the tension building between them. Neither said a word.

"Mr. Walker," broke in Professor Skye, addressing me as though he had not noticed the preceding interchange at all. "When you first saw me in the store today, where was I?"

"You were on the escalator going up to the second level," I answered, glad to have the conversation take an unemotional turn.

"And what was I doing, do you suppose?"

"Well," I answered thoughtfully, "I assumed, because you didn't want me to call out your name, that you were either helping or investigating, since that is what you do."

"You are correct," said Professor Skye. "As it happens, I was investigating. Following someone." And he turned to look at Regina Lee, startling her with this discovery.

"Professor Skye!" she exclaimed. "Why were you following me? I thought you were on my side. I thought I could trust you. I thought you wanted to help me."

Professor Skye placed his hand gently on her arm.

"And what did I tell you yesterday about the kind of help I could give you, Regina Lee?"

"That it would hurt at the time but afterward would make things better," she answered sadly.

"And so it shall," he repeated, "and so it shall. Now, tell me who *you* were following?"

I stared at Professor Skye, puzzled at just what was going on. Beside me, Regina Lee's mother did the same.

"I was following Mama," admitted Regina Lee.

Regina Lee's mother leaned forward to speak, but Professor Skye shook his head and she refrained.

"And why were you following her?" he continued.

"To see where she went," said Regina Lee, releasing only as much information as Professor Skye requested.

"Why?" he asked.

"To see what she looked at. To see what she liked," confessed Regina Lee.

"And what did she like?" asked Professor Skye. "What in particular?"

But Regina Lee shook her head and would not answer.

"Come now, Regina Lee," he urged, "you cannot have the help without the hurt. And the hurt is announcing itself in your reluctance to speak. Now once again: what particularly did you notice that your mother liked?"

Regina Lee slid closer to Professor Skye, her eyes fixed on the table surface before her. At last she spoke. "I saw her try this ring." And she raised the hand on which she wore the ring, on which her mother had commented only a little while ago.

Again Regina Lee's mother leaned forward to speak, but Professor Skye restrained her with his eyes.

"Regina Lee, why do you always wear jewelry?" continued Professor Skye with his gentle but relentless questioning.

"Because I like it," came the soft reply.

"But more than that," urged Professor Skye, pressing the truth out of her.

"Because Mama likes jewelry."

"Yes," agreed Professor Skye, "but we have two more 'whys' to

33

go. Why should your mother's fondness for jewelry cause you to want to wear it, too?"

"Because I want to be like Mama."

"This is the final 'why,' Regina Lee." Now he turned in his seat to face her.

"Why do you want to be so much like your mother?"

At this Regina Lee sucked in her breath, gathering strength for what she was about to say.

"I want to be like Mama so she will like me better," and tears were in her voice, although pride would not let them fall from her eyes. "I want her to like me as much as my brother and sisters."

"Regina Lee!" gasped her mother and reached across the table to comfort her unhappy daughter.

"Thank you, Regina Lee. You have done your part." Professor Skye leaned back as though another part remained. "And now," he said, looking at Regina Lee's mother, "I must ask your consent to finish what your daughter has bravely started. I need to ask you some questions regarding Regina Lee, questions that will be painful for you to answer and for Regina Lee to hear. However, if you will reply truthfully, I believe your concerns about your daughter will be put to rest. Shall I continue?"

Regina Lee's mother was silent, staring into the eyes of her daughter, who was staring back. She nodded without interrupting her gaze.

Then Professor Skye's gentle questioning began again. "Is it not true, as Regina Lee has said, that you are harder on her than on her sisters and her brother?"

Regina Lee's mother shook her head. "I love all my children."

"Come," insisted Professor Skye, "there is no sin in having different feelings for your different children or treating them according to their differences. As for loving your daughter, you know I was not questioning that. But unhappiness can follow where differences in valuing and treatment are misunderstood. Or when they are denied. A sad example of which you have just heard. Regina Lee has doubts about your caring for her."

"But it's not true!" protested Regina Lee's mother, speaking as much to her daughter as to Professor Skye.

"I know it's not true," he agreed. "But for Regina Lee to know this, too, there are some truths that must be told. For example, are you not harder on Regina Lee than on the other children?"

"Yes," sighed Regina Lee's mother, "I am."

"Explain why this is so."

"The children's father," she replied, "says it is because Regina Lee and I are too alike, and I would correct in her the willfulness I cannot govern in myself. He says in Regina Lee I see the child I was, with the same stubborn character, which caused me so much unhappiness and sometimes still does. I am hard on her to keep her from becoming like me." And there was a look of pleading in the mother's eyes, while those of the daughter glistened with feeling.

"So you see, Regina Lee," explained Professor Skye, "this is one reason why a parent can be unduly hard upon a child. Because they are so alike. But in your case, there is an additional reason. It is because you are also different. Is that not so?" And here Professor Skye stared intently at Regina Lee's mother, who for the first time looked away from her daughter to avoid Professor Skye's question.

"Mama, tell me! Tell me it isn't so!" Regina Lee tried desperately to re-engage her mother.

Professor Skye leaned back again, as if he could do no more.

At last Regina Lee's mother spoke. "Regina Lee, you are my darkest child."

Regina Lee nodded her head. "And that's why you care for me less," she said sadly, matter-of-factly, as though it was something she had always known but wished were not so.

"No, Child, that is why I care for you more." Now the mother locked back onto her daughter's eyes. "Your passage through life may be made more difficult for you because of that darkness, more difficult than for your brother or sisters, who have lighter skin. I am harder on you because I would have you strong. I am more critical because you must be well prepared. The world, Regina Lee, is neither kind nor just. And the darker your skin, the more cruel it can be. This is what I believe.

"Your father disagrees. He says times have changed and are still changing. But he does not argue with me, because he knows how fixed I am in my opinions. Similar to you, I am afraid." And here she smiled at Regina Lee.

"Oh, Mama, I didn't know!" and Regina Lee smiled back.

Neither smile, it seemed to me, held a lot of happiness, but both were filled with understanding. And I felt a closeness between mother and daughter that was not there when they first sat down.

"You don't have to be like me for me to love you, Regina Lee," said her mother.

"I know that, Mama. I know that now." And it seemed to me she did.

"Well," abruptly announced Regina Lee's mother. "We have taken up enough of Professor Skye's time." And for the first time she smiled at Professor Skye. Then she and Regina Lee got up from the table.

"See you, Professor Skye," said Regina Lee. "And thanks."

"You're welcome," he replied. And mother and daughter left the cafeteria walking close together.

"Now," announced Professor Skye, turning back to me, "for your question: But wasn't Regina Lee stealing from her mother?"

"Well, wasn't she?" I asked, having grown more accustomed to Professor Skye being able to read my thoughts.

"Let me ask you a question," he replied. "Assuming she was, do you believe she will continue doing it?"

I thought before I answered. "No," I finally said. "No, I don't think so."

"Then I would suggest," countered Professor Skye, "that the question of theft is no longer a useful one to consider. With the possible exception of another theft in this case: the dishonesty of Regina Lee's mother to her daughter. A theft of truth. Had these truths not been withheld so long and denied so firmly, Regina Lee would not have developed the painful conclusions that troubled her."

"I guess the moral is," I offered, "no matter how painful, it is always best to tell the truth."

"Yes," agreed Professor Skye, "that sounds like a moral all right— oversimplified and one-sided. Some day, my friend, we shall have to discuss the helpful uses of dishonesty and the damaging uses of truth. But not now. Now, I think, what I should like more than anything would be some ice cream." And he handed me a dollar. "Do me a favor. Go to the counter and bring back a dish of the best tasting ice cream they have."

"Sure," I agreed. Getting up, I went and looked over the list of flavors, and ordered strawberry ice cream. But when I turned around to bring it back, Professor Skye was gone. Left behind, on the table, was a note on a paper napkin: "Enjoy the ice cream."

So I did. And I thought about Regina Lee and her mother. And my mother. Maybe Mom was extra hard on me, not because she didn't love me, but because she did. Because I was different from her and my sister.

My sister! When I got back, I told her all about the big chunks of juicy strawberries in the ice cream and how good they were.

"Big deal! Who cares?" she said.

But I could tell she did by how she asked my mom for ice cream right away. Of course, Mom said, "No." No dessert till after supper, which my sister argued wasn't fair.

And I said, "Big deal! Who cares?"

And she said, she wasn't asking me for my opinion. And now Saturday at home was turning out a whole lot better than it began.

# CHAPTER FOUR

## A Case of Loyalty

The next week was our first visit with Dad and Marie since they got married, and, boy, was Mom upset. We could tell by how she swore nothing was wrong but kept complaining about every little thing.

I told my sister I thought Mom was angry at us for going, and my sister agreed because she was angry, too.

"If he thinks he can leave our family and have me help him start another, he's crazy. I'm not going! Why should I do something to please him that will only hurt Mom? Hasn't he hurt everyone enough already?"

I thought my sister was right, except I wanted to keep seeing Dad because I missed him a lot. I'd only see him occasionally since the divorce, and then just for a weekend. We spent the time doing lots of fun things, but no matter how much fun we had, it still felt sad. And no matter how we tried, we couldn't make being together feel as good as when he was still at home. Maybe we tried too hard.

Besides, he was different now. At least in how he looked and what he liked to do. He was much thinner, and he was into exercise and sports. He never exercised when he and Mom were married. He just complained about his weight. She said he changed because of Marie. She said that's what happens when an older man marries a younger woman. I don't know. Except we did a lot of outdoor stuff we never did before.

What a fix! If I saw Dad and Marie, I'd hurt Mom. If I refused, like my sister, I'd hurt Dad. Either way, I'd get hurt. Here was a problem even Professor Skye couldn't solve. Professor Skye. It had been a while since I'd seen him last at Bolster's. Who knew when I might see him again? Not this afternoon for sure, because

I had to stay home to show the repairman the damage from the water leak, while Mom and my sister went shopping and then took in a movie.

Usually, I like staying home alone. No sister to bug me, no mom to boss me around. But it was Sunday, and I was getting tired of being trapped indoors. At last the doorbell rang. Maybe if the problem got fixed fast enough, I'd still have time to play outside. So I hurried to let the person in.

"Professor Skye! What are you doing here?"

"I came to fix the leak and replace some plumbing," answered Professor Skye. "You've been expecting me."

"No," I explained. "I've been expecting the repairman, not you."

"As you wish," said Professor Skye. "Now give me a hand with this toolbox and show me where the trouble is. We haven't got much time before our next case arrives."

Without asking what he meant, although I would have liked to, I led him to the kitchen, which was still a mess. Everything was put up off the floor, and wet towels were soaking underneath the counters where the mop couldn't reach.

"It flooded everywhere before Mom figured out how to shut the water off," I said. "Then she called the landlord."

"She did," agreed Professor Skye, "and then he called a friend of mine, who called me."

"Is this your job?" I asked. "How did you learn?"

"I make my living here and there," replied Professor Skye, peering under the sink with a flashlight. "Give me the red wrench."

I handed him the tool he wanted. He kept talking while he worked.

"When you're free of money, you learn to do things for yourself, or else they don't get done. The less you have, the more you learn to do. So I've learned to do a lot."

I watched as he unscrewed the joint and twisted the pipes apart.

"Of course, fixing things is different from fixing people. People don't come with directions, and there's no ordering spare parts. You have to work with what you have and figure what to do as you go along. Now hand me those two curved pieces of pipe."

It didn't take him long to replace the plumbing and refit the joint.

"There," he announced. "That should do it. Now, while I go and turn the water on, you bring the chairs back in, so we can all sit around the kitchen table."

"We?" I asked, but he had left the room. So I arranged the chairs and wondered who he meant. "We?" I asked again when he returned.

"Yes. You and I. Eldridge and Lamar. And of course, Big Sally."

"Of course," I agreed, not seeing how such a crowd was going to fit in our small kitchen.

"A hard problem, loyalty," began Professor Skye, sitting down on one of the chairs. "Particularly when it becomes divided. Eldridge feels torn. He loves his older brother, and he loves his mother, and he wants to do what's right. But what is right for one is wrong for the other. If he tells Lamar's secret, then Lamar will be angry at him. If he keeps it, then, when she finds out, his mother will be even angrier. Your job will be to help him out of this dilemma."

"My job?" I asked, not wanting the responsibility. "Why is it my job? How would I know how to help him with his problem?"

"You wouldn't," replied Professor Skye, lowering his voice. "Not at first. Neither would I. Fortunately, we don't have to have answers to help people find solutions. Just follow the problem along, see what you notice, and maybe you'll discover something that can be of use."

"But," I protested, "I don't want to be a helper!"

Just then the doorbell rang.

Professor Skye sat back, as comfortable as I was not.

"Aren't you going to see who it is?" he asked.

The bell rang again. I shook my head in frustration. I wanted to answer it, but I didn't want to let the problem in.

This time the bell rang twice. Oh, the heck with it!

"I'm coming!" I called, at last leaving the kitchen. There was no turning back now.

Opening the front door, I saw two boys on the steps, one older than my sister, the other younger than me.

43

"Is Professor Skye around?" asked the younger. "He said to meet him here."

"So I did," greeted a voice behind me. "Eldridge, right on time. And you must be Lamar. I'm Professor Skye."

The older boy nodded slightly, scowled, said nothing, and looked sullen.

"And this," announced Professor Skye, glancing at me, "is my associate, Mr. Olive Green. Why don't you both join us in the kitchen."

I wanted to say that wasn't my name, but Professor Skye had turned back down the hall, so the rest of us just followed. Now there were soft drinks on the table by each of the five chairs and a plate of cookies in the middle.

Sitting down, Professor Skye passed the cookies and then turned to Lamar: "I'm glad you came. I wasn't sure you would."

Lamar chewed slowly and didn't say a word, but I could see the muscles in his jaw biting down harder than the cookie needed.

"If I were you," continued Professor Skye, "I might be mad at Eldridge for arranging this meeting. How did he get you here?"

Something about Professor Skye's insistence was hard to refuse. It made you talk when you didn't want to.

"He threatened to rat on me unless I came. He better not if he knows what's good for him!" He shot an angry glare at Eldridge, who hung his head but shook it at the same time.

"You're in trouble and you know it!" said the younger boy.

"Nothing I can't handle. Some brother you are, messing in my business! Going to tell Mom!"

"And if your mother was told," interrupted Professor Skye, "what would happen?"

Lamar bit his lip. "She'd ship me off. When she says 'one more time,' she means it."

"How would that be for Eldridge, do you think?" asked Professor Skye.

"Probably what he wants. To get rid of me!"

"You know that's not true! You and Mom are the only family I've got here!"

Now it was Lamar's turn to hang his head.

"Better you be sent away to relatives than be sent to jail. I'm only trying to help." Eldridge sounded sad. "Besides, Mom would want to know."

"She doesn't need to know everything. I thought I could trust you!"

"Professor Skye," Eldridge was starting to sound desperate. "You said you'd help me. What should I do?"

"Ask Mr. Green," said Professor Skye.

"Him?" asked Eldridge, looking over at me.

Professor Skye nodded.

What I was afraid of. Professor Skye was putting me on the spot again.

"What should I do?" Eldridge repeated the question at me.

What should *I* do? I wondered to myself. Then, seeing that Professor Skye was going to leave whatever happened up to me, I plunged ahead. "Maybe it's not so bad," I said, trying to make Eldridge feel better. Then I asked Lamar, "Is it so bad?"

"Not yet," he answered.

Both brothers were treating me like I knew where the conversation was going.

"But it could be?" I asked Lamar.

"Yeah," he admitted. "It depends on the other guys. If I join in what they want to do."

"How come Eldridge knows?" I was curious.

"'Cause I told him."

"Why?"

"He needs to know what can happen. I'm his older brother. I look out for him. No sense him making my mistakes."

"So it is a mistake?" I asked.

"Yeah. But it's too late now. I gave my word."

Then it occurred to me: "Now it sounds like Eldridge is trying to look after you. Getting you in trouble with your mom to keep you out of trouble with your friends."

"I guess so." And the look Lamar gave his younger brother wasn't as hostile anymore.

"Thank you, Mr. Green," interrupted Professor Skye. "You've done almost enough for one day. Just one thing more: go and let Big Sally in."

"Huh?" I asked. "No one's ringing."

Just then there came a loud knocking on the door. I looked at Professor Skye and just shook my head.

"I'll go get her," I said.

Professor Skye smiled. "You do that."

So I did because I didn't want to keep the lady waiting. Except it turned out not be a lady after all. Instead, an enormous policeman filled the doorway.

"You're not a girl!" I blurted out in surprise.

The big man laughed. "Not since last I looked. Professor Skye here?"

I pointed down the hall to the kitchen, but he let me know I was supposed to lead the way.

"Hey, Sarge, what's happening?" the policeman greeted Professor Skye.

"Just minding other people's business, Big Sally, like always. Glad you could make it. Gentlemen," Professor Skye declared, looking at Eldridge, Lamar, and me, "this is Officer LaSalle, here to help with the last part of our problem. Big Sally, this is . . ." But Officer LaSalle interrupted the introductions.

"Sarge, no need for names since we're not talking about anybody here. Just old Tyrone. What kind of trouble's he in now?"

"Yes, Big Sally, Tyrone it is," agreed Professor Skye. He looked at the three of us to make sure we understood. "Tyrone's got himself in another jam all right. Lamar, you know Tyrone better than the rest of us. Tell Officer LaSalle what's going down."

Lamar coughed like something was sticking in his throat.

"Want me to tell?" asked Eldridge.

"I can do it!" growled Lamar, seeing that if he didn't, his brother would. "It's nothing yet. Just plans is all. Except I —except Tyrone gave his word he'd go along. Back out now and they won't be his friends."

"How come Tyrone gives his word to something he don't want to do?" asked Officer LaSalle.

46

Lamar shook his head.

"One minute they were all hanging out with nothing to do. Next thing they were all excited about this idea, and he'd agreed."

"That sounds like old Tyrone, all right," said Officer LaSalle. "Sometimes he ain't wrapped too tight. Thinks with his mouth instead of his head. Suppose we get him out of this fix. How do we know he won't get into another one just like it?"

"He won't," promised Lamar. "He gave me his word."

"That's good enough for me," said Officer LaSalle. He turned toward Professor Skye. "Hey, Sarge, remember how you stopped the enemy attack without even firing a shot?"

Professor Skye nodded. "Got word to them through the underground that we knew they were coming. Spoiled their surprise, so they called it off."

"Yeah, what I was thinking," said Officer LaSalle. "I might do the same thing now. Drop a few words in the right places for Tyrone's friends to pick up. About what I've been hearing on the street. Nothing official. But maybe enough so walking into where they'd be expected isn't what they want to do." He stood up.

"Break's over. Time to get back to work. I'll drop you two along the way."

Eldridge and Lamar got up, too.

"Thanks, Professor Skye," said Eldridge.

"I guess so," murmured Lamar.

All three left for the front door.

"Your place?" called Officer LaSalle.

"My place," answered Professor Skye. "Later."

I heard the front door close.

Professor Skye was watching me closely. "The question you want to ask," he began, "is: Why did Big Sally call me Sarge?"

"Well, why did he?" I asked.

"Because a war ago, I was his sergeant."

"Did you fight together?"

"We did."

"Did you want to go to war?" I was trying to picture Professor Skye as a soldier. "Did you wear that jacket?"

"No and yes," he replied. "Yes, I wore this jacket. No, I didn't want to go. I didn't believe in the war, but I didn't believe in refusing to serve my country, either."

"So you went and decided to believe in the war after all," I said.

"No," he answered. "I decided to fight in a war I didn't believe in. Like Eldridge, I was torn between two wrongs. Like him, I finally decided that my first loyalty was not to one choice or the other, but to myself. To do what felt right for me." He looked at his watch. "Now, while I pack these cans up, why don't you dump that paper plate in the trash out back. You can finish up the last two cookies as you go."

I picked up the plate and went out the kitchen door to the garbage cans. Munching the cookies, I suddenly remembered how I wanted to ask Professor Skye about whether I should go visit Dad and Marie.

But when I got back inside, Professor Skye was gone. Now what was I going to do? Either way Mom or Dad was going to feel bad. Then I thought about what Professor Skye had asked himself: What felt right for him? So I asked myself the same question. And the answer seemed clear. I wanted to see Dad, just like I wanted to see Mom. The important thing for me was to see them both.

Straightening the chairs around the table, I heard the front door open and my mom came in. First she looked under the sink, then at me.

"Looks like you've been entertaining," she said.

"Sure," I told the truth. "I had Professor Skye and three other guys over. We all sat around the table and talked."

"Now don't you start telling stories again," she scolded.

"All right," I promised. "I won't." And I didn't.

# CHAPTER FIVE

## A Case of Jealousy

The first visit with Dad and Marie went okay, even though it didn't start out very well. When they came to pick me up, Mom broke down and cried. And my sister cried, too, except she refused to come out of the house. Then, when Dad tried to comfort Mom, it only made her worse. She got angry and told them both to take me and leave, and have me back on time. What a mess!

The three of us were pretty quiet in the car. I felt unhappy and wished Marie hadn't come along. She must have heard my wish because I heard her whisper to my dad that next time it would be best for him to come alone.

When we got to their apartment, Dad and I went off biking for an hour. Marie had supper fixed when we got back. It was the first time she and I had to talk. She wasn't how my sister said she'd be—mean and ordering me around, keeping me from time with Dad. Mostly she was friendly, without being pushy. And when we played games that night, she was fun and funny. She liked to laugh and I do, too.

After Dad dropped me back home, Mom asked about my visit, so I told her it was great, because it was. I thought she would be pleased, but instead she gave me a funny look I hadn't seen before, almost like she was suspicious. Then she wanted to hear everything we did, all about the apartment and Marie. Like, was Marie a good cook? When I said she was, Mom suddenly got up and left. Then my sister came running in to read me out, angry 'cause I got Mom all upset. I did? I didn't mean to. All I did was answer her questions. If she didn't want to know, why did she ask?

"Boy, are you stupid!" my sister said, and I guess I was. Except it was hard figuring how to tell Mom enough without saying too much.

One part of the problem Mom quickly solved. Dad wasn't going to pick me up at the house anymore. Or drop me off there. If she didn't have to see him, she'd get less upset when I was going to have my time with him. So she decided I was going to learn to ride the bus, which was all right by me because I enjoyed getting out on my own.

Practice first, my mom ordered, and study before I practiced. She sat me down with the bus route map and schedules. She made me memorize the stops and the change I would need to make to get where Dad would meet me. Backward and forward until she was sure I understood each way.

Next Saturday was set for practice. I could have till four o'clock in the afternoon to ride around and get confident traveling by myself. She gave me three dollars so I could buy some lunch at the Central Terminal, and some change to call if I wanted her to pick me up.

"I hope you get lost!" my sister said.

I could tell she was jealous, and I would have tried to get her back, except Mom had told me my sister was too mad at Dad to see him, and too sad not to miss him. I was *not* to tease her about this, did I understand? So instead of saying something smart like "I hope you have fun staying home," I said nothing.

Mom walked me to the stop, and the bus came right on time.

"Remember, you can call me. I'll be near the phone all day."

I gave her a hug, climbed on board, and paid my money as the bus pulled away. I wanted to sit by the window if I could.

"Over here," called a familiar voice. And there, farther down the aisle, sat Professor Skye.

"Professor Skye! Where are you going?"

"I saved you a seat by the window," he said, standing up to let me in. "Where are *we* going, you mean," he gently corrected. "We are going where I can get some help."

"You?" I asked. "I thought you only gave help."

"Every helper needs help sometimes. That's why every helper needs a teacher," he explained. "We are going to see mine. The case in hand I can't solve by myself."

"You have a teacher?" I was surprised.

"Yes."

"And does your teacher have a teacher, too?"

"Of course. Every beginning helper must find a teacher," he said.

"Except you found me." Now it was my turn to correct him.

"Did I?" he asked.

"Sure. Don't you remember. I was sitting down, and you came and sat down next to me."

"No," he said. "I don't remember that. What I remember is your sitting down beside me on the curb, so preoccupied with your own thoughts that at first you didn't notice me at all."

But before I could object, he stood up.

"Here is where we change," he announced, and we got off. "Do you know where we are?"

I did, from being taught by Mom.

"Some of your memory's improving. Good," he said. "Now we take this next bus to the end of the line."

Settling back for a longer ride, I tried to let my thoughts wander over the sights that rolled past the window, but my mind got stuck instead.

"The question you want to ask," interrupted Professor Skye, "is: What name am I going to give you today, and why?"

He was right. The signs I had been reading caused me to wonder about names, and then about the names he was always giving me."

"Well," I asked. "Why do you give me made-up names and not my own?"

"To help you set yourself aside," he answered, lowering his voice. "How you are can get in the way of seeing how other people are, which can get in the way of giving help. For example, if you were very shy and lonely, you might see other people as distant and uncaring."

"Like when I'm feeling angry at my sister," I said, "I think she's out to get me even when she's not."

"Exactly. So I give you an unusual name to help you stop being your usual self. So you can focus clearly on the person we are trying to help."

I was glad Professor Skye had a reason for giving me these silly-sounding names. But I really didn't see how I could just give up being the person I was, and said so.

"Yes," he agreed. "It's distance we are after, not divorce. To get distance is why we're going to see my old teacher today. Before I can help Reuben and Teresa get untangled, I must get untangled myself."

"Your teacher must be a smart man," I said.

"Must he?" asked Professor Skye. "Well, soon you can decide for yourself. Last stop." Then we got off.

It was mostly quiet streets with small houses, nothing fancy, almost like country. We must have walked four or five blocks when a little brown puppy, following its nose, ran out of a yard and bumped into my leg. It looked surprised to see me and wagged its tail. I stopped to pick it up and carried it back to the owner, a short, stubby woman with long gray hair pinned up on her head, who sat on the stoop petting an old fat cat.

"He like you," she said. "He don't like everyone. Who's your friend?"

"That's Professor Skye," I answered. "We were just walking by when your dog ran out."

"Hey, you!" she called at Professor Skye, who was lounging at the gate. "Come here!"

Professor Skye shambled up the path.

"Well," she demanded. "You have something to say for your-self?"

I thought Professor Skye looked kind of embarrassed.

"I suppose you want the truth," he mumbled at last.

"I don't want no poor excuse, that's for sure!" she replied.

He shrugged, resigned to tell her what he didn't want to tell.

"Sosa, I've been busy with my work."

"Busy? You been busy, Jackson? Too busy to visit your old teacher? Your work more important than seeing me?"

By saying nothing, Professor Skye admitted that it was.

"You lucky I'm no jealous woman, Jackson, or I tear your heart out. Not like Diabla here," patting the cat. "She don't like this puppy one darn bit. But what am I to do? People don't have money, but they want to pay me. So they give me what they can. What they

**54**

grow, what they make, and this puppy here. He came yesterday, and ever since Diabla never leave my lap. Puppy try climb up and she scratch him good. He don't try again." Sosa looked at me. "Here, Amado, you," she said.

"Me? Amado?" Now I was being given a new name by her!

"What? You don't like the name? It was good enough for my husband, it's good enough for you. Now sit. Make a place." And she lifted up Diabla and slid her into my lap. "You pet her good while I pet the puppy. See, she stay with you but don't take her eyes off him." Soon the puppy fell asleep and at last the cat looked away and began to knead my lap with her paws. She started purring.

"So, Jackson, you come. Why you come? I know. You got yourself into a case you can't get out. You only come for help. Not to see me."

Professor Skye hung his head.

"I'm an ungrateful student, back for one more lesson of instruction, " he confessed.

"No, Jackson. You no ungrateful. You just love your work too much. I taught you that, so I should know. Now, tell Sosa."

And she lifted up the puppy and pushed him gently into my lap beside Diabla, who stirred but stayed, as I began to pet them both.

Professor Skye sat down upon the stoop.

"Sosa, Reuben and Teresa, you should see them. Like Selma and myself at that age. So much in love they can hardly stand each other. Fighting all the time. Too much together and they fight to be apart. Too much apart and they fight because they're not together. They want to get married, but not if they can't find a way to stop the fighting. It goes on all the time."

"What they afraid of?" asked Sosa.

"Of losing each other, what else? That's why they act so possessive."

"Yes, like you and Selma," said Sosa, putting her hand on his arm. "Held on so tight you drove the other one away. No other woman for you, eh, Jackson?"

Professor Skye looked very sad. He sighed and shook his head.

"No. My first love and my last. Why, I don't want Reuben and Teresa to lose each other."

"They say they can't help fighting?" asked Sosa.

"Yes. They don't even know how the fights start anymore. Neither do I. What can I tell them?"

"To fight, of course. To fight some more."

What? I thought. This sounded crazy.

Professor Skye thought so, too. "Sosa, they fight too much already."

"No, Jackson. They fight without knowing how fighting starts. So they don't know what they are doing. You tell them Sosa says, twice a day. At 6:00 in the morning and at 6:00 at night. They have to fight whether they want or not. Say if they want fighting to stop, they must practice fighting first. For one week. Is the best way."

Professor Skye smiled. "I never thought of that," he said. "If they can plan and practice how to do it, I guess they can learn how it happens and choose not to do it. I'll tell them. And I'll let you know how they come out."

"No, Jackson. Not you. You won't let Sosa know. You'll forget until next time you need her. That's okay. Someday the student has to let the teacher go. Even Amado here." She looked at me.

"You do pretty good, you know that? Teach Diabla what she needs to know. Is room in lap for two, eh? So you don't be jealous anymore, Diabla." She was talking now to the cat, who awoke and appeared to listen. "This little dog don't take none of your space in Sosa's heart. Plenty for everyone. Now," she spoke to me again, "you put them back into Sosa's lap. The puppy first, and then Diabla. There." And they rolled together in the hammock of her skirt, the puppy licking the cat, the cat not minding.

Professor Skye got up.

"Thank you, Sosa. Maybe with your help Reuben and Teresa will make it after all."

"You. What about you, Jackson? What about Selma? So many years ago, and still each time you think of her, inside you cry. Why you don't let her go?"

Professor Skye smiled, but it was not a happy smile.

"Because I'd rather hold onto her memory than not have her at all."

56

"As you want, Jackson. But watch out. Dream of her too much and she becomes a dream."

"My choice, Sosa. To make her as wonderful as I want to remember."

Sosa shook her head, then looked at me.

"What you think, Amado, of a man like this, eh? He make himself feel unhappy to feel happy. He make no sense."

Like Professor Skye, now Sosa was putting me on the spot, both of them awaiting my reply.

"Sometimes people act mixed up," I spoke at last, thinking about Mom wanting me to have a good time with Dad and Marie, and then feeling sorry when I did. "It's confusing. But sometimes they want what they don't want. And I think maybe that's okay."

"Maybe so, Amado, maybe so. Is okay with you, Jackson?"

"It's okay with me, Sosa."

"Then go," she said. "But don't forget your lunches." And she handed each of us a bag from underneath the stoop.

Professor Skye laughed. "You were expecting us!"

"Of course, why you surprised? Who teach you how to know without being told? Do you think Sosa has no better to do than sit in the sun? I was waiting. You were on time. Now get along. Sosa has work to do."

On the first leg of the bus ride home we didn't say much. Just ate the lunch Sosa had provided. I wondered if scheduling fights with my sister would stop our fighting.

"No," announced Professor Skye, interrupting my thoughts. "It would only make the fighting worse. Getting each other and getting each other back is what you both like. When one begins to lose interest is when the fighting will begin to end. Now, do you know where we are?"

I recognized the name of the stop and stood up to get off and change. I thought Professor Skye was hurrying right behind me, but he must have stayed on, because when I looked around he and the bus were gone.

I didn't have to wait long until my next bus arrived, getting home before Mom had to start worrying. She was glad to see me.

57

"I really missed you, too," said my sister, not meaning it.

"And I missed you," I said, not meaning it back.

And Mom put us both to work because she was in no mood to hear our bickering. Plus she treated me kind of distantly, the way she had when I came back from my visit with Dad and Marie. And I didn't like it.

So, later on that night, when she was tucking me in bed, I was trying to think of what I could say, when I thought of Sosa. I said: "You know, Mom, I have room in my heart for everyone. For you *and* Dad. Even for Marie, even though she can never be my mom."

Suddenly she got a funny look in her eyes, which wasn't funny, and she began to cry. "Now what made you say that?" she asked.

"I don't know." If I couldn't convince her of Professor Skye, I sure couldn't get her to believe in Sosa.

"Well, you're right. I guess I've just been feeling scared. And I don't need to." Then she gave me a hug and went over to tuck my sister in and give her a hug, too. Turning out the light, she closed the door.

"Sweet dreams," she called.

"See!" whispered my sister at me. "See what you've done! You've got her upset again. She's crying!"

But my sister was wrong. I thought of Professor Skye.

"Not all unhappiness is sad," I said.

# CHAPTER SIX

## A Case of Lying

Now that I was riding the bus back and forth every other weekend to see Dad and Marie, my leaving and coming home were less upsetting to my mom. Except she would still ask about my visit: How was it? I didn't like the question, but I liked my answer even less. I lied. I made it sound like seeing Dad and Marie was just okay, when it was really lots of fun. Dad was happier to be around than when he used to live at home, and I was getting to enjoy being with Marie.

She didn't act like a stepmother, bossing me around. The most she ever did was ask. Plus she wasn't near as old as Dad. She was as close to my age as she was to his. More like a much older sister, except much nicer than the one I had. Easy to talk to. And she liked to joke.

Of course, I couldn't tell Mom. That really would hurt her feelings. But I didn't like to lie because it made me feel as if I was hiding something wrong, when I wasn't. And then I had to worry about her finding out. I felt awkward with Mom when I wanted to feel close. It reminded me of something Professor Skye had said after we helped Regina Lee. About how not all dishonesty was bad. But it felt bad, and he hadn't told me that. I don't mean lying to my sister. That was okay. That didn't matter. Besides, it served her right for treating me like a traitor each time I made a visit. It seemed like she got more and more angry as time went on. While Mom, when she talked about the divorce, was sounding less angry than confused.

"I just can't think why your father left," she'd say over and over again, puzzled, like she was searching for an answer. "We weren't unhappy, at least I never thought we were. He never said anything. If we talked, mostly it was about you kids. Just an ordinary marriage. I didn't know anything was wrong."

I didn't either. They were kind of boring together, but I just figured most parents were. And I never saw them fight, until the end. Then she pleaded for him not to go, and he didn't want to hear what she had to say. That was then. Now the worst was over, at least for me. No more of their fighting. She wasn't mad all the time. And here was a long weekend coming up 'cause Monday was a holiday. Just what I liked. Free time. With the weeks so busy and the little house so crowded, time by myself was hard to come by.

Mom offered to take both of us to a movie, but I said, "No," they could go. I'd rather bum around the neighborhood and maybe find a friend.

"What friend?" Mom asked, because so far I hadn't made any.

I didn't have a good answer, since all the kids who lived close by were much younger than me.

"I don't know," I said. "Maybe I just want to be alone outside."

"All right." Mom gave permission. "But stay in the neighborhood."

"Maybe he's going to play with his friend, Professor Skye," teased my sister. Even Mom smiled.

"Maybe I will!" I retorted, feeling the old anger at not being believed, then feeling frustrated because I had no way to meet him even if I wanted.

"Liar, liar, pants on fire!" singsonged my sister.

"Stop it!" ordered Mom. "Come along or we'll be late." And off they went to the movie.

They had spoiled my good time by leaving me in a bad mood. I stuck around the house and made myself a snack, but that didn't help. So at last I went outside and started walking up the sidewalk, counting cracks and measuring steps, two steps to a square, figuring how many squares to a block.

"You wanted to see me?" asked a familiar voice.

I looked up. There was Professor Skye, walking toward me.

"Professor Skye! I didn't know how to reach you."

"Yes, you did," he disagreed, "or you wouldn't have found me as quickly as you did. And a good thing, too, knowing Jessalyn. The more time we give her, the more trouble she'll be into." And he increased his stride till I was rushing to keep up.

62

Around the corner we hurried, down four blocks, across the street, down three more blocks, finally turning into the dark alley behind San Gabriel Elementary School, a place students were told they weren't supposed to go.

Speeding toward us was a small girl on a bicycle, riding on just the rear wheel, lifting the front one off the ground. I wasn't sure she saw us, but she did and skidded to a sudden stop inches from where Professor Skye was standing. Maybe eight or nine years old, she had a wild gleam in her eye and a reckless smile on her face, which disappeared as soon as the excitement from the trick was over. In a moment, her expression became serious and sad.

"Hi, Professor Skye," she said and then looked curiously at me.

"Hi, Jessalyn. This is my friend, Mr. Ali Kabar. He knows a lot about lying, so I brought him along."

What? Lying? Why did every case we have always have something to do with me?

There were some overturned barrels, and the three of us sat down on those. Jessalyn was as talkative as she was active. She couldn't stay still and she couldn't keep silent. At least not for long.

"Professor Skye, I promised my sister I'd be home in an hour. She's keeping us today, and she's worse than my parents. Being late means getting popped. She won't listen to my stories, so I don't even try to make one up."

Then she spoke to me. "How come you know so much about lying?"

What a question! What was I supposed to be, some kind of expert? But I knew Professor Skye wasn't going to rescue me.

"I have to lie to my mom now," I explained, "or else her feelings will get hurt."

"Yeah, I know what you mean," Jessalyn agreed. "Same with me. If I told my mom and dad everything I did or tried to do, they'd be freaked out all the time."

"What do you try to do?" I asked.

"Dangerous stuff. I never turn down a dare. Climbing, keeping my balance on high places, seeing how fast I can go. Stuff like that. I told my mom the scare was half the fun, but she said, no, it wasn't. Not for her. And I better not. My dad agreed because he doesn't like me getting Mom upset. So I started lying to her when I did. And she believed me, except when I would come back hurt. Then I'd say I learned my lesson this time and I won't do it again. And she'd say, did I promise? And I said, 'cross my heart.' But all the time I was thinking up my next adventure. I can't help it. That's just the way I am. The way Dad says he was as a kid, but I better not be like him."

"So now what happens when she catches you?" I was curious.

"She makes me stay inside, which she knows I hate. But she hates it, too, because she has to stay inside and watch me. If she leaves, she thinks I'll leave once she has gone. And I will, unless my dad is there, 'cause that's just how I've always been for as long as both of them remember. 'Daredevil,' they call me. Then Mom will shake her head and say, God must have saved her worst child for last. And Dad will say, it must be justice, to get a kid who was just like him. Maybe so. I don't mean to be worst. I just want to do what I want to do. The scarier, the better."

"So how come you bother to lie," I asked, "if you're going to do what you want anyway?"

"That's easy. If I'm going to get punished for what I do, I might as well try to see if I can get away with it. But it's getting harder."

"How come?"

"Because Mom and Dad aren't fooled so easily anymore. And now I've started lying about other things. About stupid things. I don't mean to, but I do it all the time. Particularly with Mom. She asks me anything and out slips a lie. Without even thinking. That's what I was telling Professor Skye. Lying about one thing has got me lying about others."

Professor Skye nodded but said nothing, leaving me to carry on the conversation with Jessalyn.

"You sound like you can't stop doing it," I said.

"I can't." Jessalyn looked scared. "The more I lie, the more I lie. I cover up one lie with another, and pretty soon I can't remember every lie I've told. How am I supposed to keep them all straight? I lose track of what I've said and feel out of control. That's when she trips me up. But by then I've told so many lies, I'm frightened of the truth. So I lie. I say that I'm not lying, even though she knows

I am. Then she gets angry and leaves, and I'm left all alone. I want to get back close with her, but all the lies I've told are in the way. But how can I be honest? If she knew all my lies, she'd think I'm even worse than she does now!"

Something wasn't sounding right. Jessalyn wasn't being Jessalyn was how I felt, so that is what I said. "How can someone who loves doing scary things not do something they want because they're scared? Go on," I challenged Jessalyn, "tell your mom the truth. I dare you!"

Wow! You should have seen her face when I said that. It hardened up. Her mouth got tight and her eyes got real focused, like she was getting herself ready to take some enormous risk.

"Thank you, Mr. Kabar," interrupted Professor Skye.

"Except it's not that simple," objected Jessalyn. "Daring myself to tell the truth won't stop some lies from slipping out from habit."

"That's right," agreed Professor Skye. "So if you can't catch a lie before you tell it, you must catch it after it's been told. And correct it."

"That's even harder than telling the truth to begin with," said Jessalyn. "Telling Mom or Dad what I told them was a lie!"

But I could see from her expression that the difficulty appealed to Jessalyn. She looked eager and excited. Almost like she couldn't wait to get home and try being honest for a change.

"Got to go!" she announced, mounting her bike. Then, spinning her back wheel, she took off like a shot.

"See you 'round, Professor Skye," she called.

"See you around, Jessalyn," he called back.

I watched her take a hard turn at the end of the alley, almost taking a spill, jamming down her leg to keep from falling, righting herself at the last minute. Then she was gone, full speed ahead.

"Your question is," interrupted Professor Skye, "Do I think Jessalyn will tell her mother and father nothing but the truth from here on out?"

"Well, will she?"

"No," replied Professor Skye. "No child always tells her parents the truth, any more than any parents are always honest with their child. Jessalyn was right. With practice, lying can become a habit.

But so can truth. However, contrary to what you may have heard, practice does not make perfect. Most of the time is as often as most people can tell the truth. And now for your next question. Do you want to ask it or shall I?"

"You can," I said.

"Why didn't I tell you that even when you're lying to do good, you can end up feeling bad?"

"Well, why didn't you?" I asked.

"Because I wanted you to learn that even at best, lying leads to harm. Jessalyn started lying to keep her parents from being scared and to protect herself from being caught. But she ended up lying more than she wanted, feeling distant from her mom, and feeling worse about herself. Sooner or later, lying harms the liar more than those to whom the lies are told. Even good lies are costly."

I thought about me and Mom when he said this, and how I lied about my visits.

"Perhaps it's time for you to go home," he suggested.

"Yeah, they should be there by now," I agreed.

"Do you remember the way?"

"Sure," I answered, leading him down the alley. But when I turned the corner and looked around, Professor Skye was gone.

My sister was glad to see me.

"You missed a great movie and a giant popcorn with lots of butter," she teased, hoping I would want to tease her back and we could fight.

But I was growing tired of fighting with my sister. It wasn't fun anymore because she was angry all the time. So I niced her instead: "Good. I'm glad you had a good time." And she left me alone after that.

Then the phone rang. It was Henry for my mom. "Henery" is what my sister and I decided to name him.

"Hey Mom! It's Henery," I called.

"Henry," she corrected, shook her head, and took the phone. Some guy that she had met at work a while ago. Now he called her or she called him every night.

Later, when Mom was sitting on my bed, I decided to tell her the truth.

"Sometimes," I began, "I have a better time with Dad and Marie than I let on."

"I know," she answered. "And I appreciate your not telling me."

"You're not mad at me for having fun and lying about it?"

"You don't have to lie," she smiled. "Maybe it's better if I just don't ask about your visit. Or maybe I need to ask a different question: Are you glad to see me when you get back?"

"Sure. I'm always glad to see you. You're my mom!"

"That's all I really need to know," and she gave me a hug. Then her face grew serious.

"I've got something to confess to you about your dad and me," she said. "Why he left. I think I'm beginning to understand. We weren't unhappy, that was true. But we weren't happy, either. Just two good people doing the best we could without any joy in what we did. So when he met Marie, I believe he saw a chance for happiness and took it. Even though it hurt a lot, I can see why."

Then she started to cry, and I gave her a hug. But my sister, who had been listening from the other bed, got angry: "That's no good reason to divorce! At least not when you have kids. Anyway, I don't care!"

But I think she was lying. Because people don't get angry over what they don't care about.

# CHAPTER SEVEN

## A Case of Anger

Just when I thought things were getting better, they got worse. School started calling Mom about my sister. First, it was not paying attention in class. Then it was not completing tests. Then it was not doing homework. Then it was refusing to obey the teacher. Then it was for talking back. That's when she was sent to the office and the Assistant Principal called Mom.

What a scene we had that night! Mom was hot when she got home, but so was my sister.

"Yes, you will!"

"No, I won't!"

Back and forth, each one getting madder, until Mom had to leave the room or else she'd say something she'd be sorry for later.

That's when my sister started to cry, and I could see she wasn't really angry. She was hurt.

I asked her what was wrong, but she told me to shut up, mind my own business, and leave her alone! But thanks for asking.

Thanks? My sister never thanked me for anything. What was going on?

Then Mom strode back in, calmed down, with her mind made up.

"All right, you don't have to tell me what's going on. But I have something to tell you. Tomorrow, you and I and all your teachers and the counselor are going to meet after school to talk about what's happening and see what can be done."

"I don't care!" declared my sister defiantly, like she was going on strike and whatever anybody did no longer mattered. But I guess some of it did, because at the meeting Mom offered to take time off her job to sit in class and watch my sister take her tests and follow directions and do her work. And my sister got furious. Afterward, she told Mom that was the stupidest idea: did she want to embarrass my sister in front of all her friends? And Mom explained she didn't want to take time off from work, but she was *willing* to if my sister couldn't take care of business at school. And she wasn't trying to embarrass her, only to help get the schoolwork done.

And speaking of homework, which my sister wasn't, Mom said that if it didn't all come home and all get done and all get turned in, at the end of the next day she would start coming up to school and they would get the assignments from the teachers. Walk down the hall *together* room by room and pick them up. And the following morning she would accompany my sister to school to make sure it all got turned in. All of it. Did my sister understand?

It was all-out war, with Mom winning the battle over schoolwork, but my sister winning when it came to anger. She would barely talk to Mom, and when she did, it was in a snarling tone of voice, so Mom didn't much like talking to her. Which I guess is why my sister started talking to me. Even though I was her brother, I was better than no one.

But it was sad. Mom and my sister had always been best friends, and now they were acting like enemies.

"Tomorrow your sister and I will be late getting home," Mom announced. "We have another conference at school."

"I can hardly wait!" growled my sister.

But Mom ignored the sarcasm. Letting my sister have her say was okay, so long as Mom got her way.

Next afternoon, all by myself at home, I was feeling gloomy about how unhappy everybody was. I stared out the front window at the street. No traffic. Not a single person. Nothing. If only Professor Skye could help me now!

What? A moment ago no one, and now Professor Skye was there, sitting where I first met him, on the curb. I ran out of the house.

"Professor Skye!" I exclaimed.

He glanced around. "You're getting better at finding me," he said.

"I didn't find you," I explained. "I wished for you."

"Same thing," he replied. "I hope you're battle ready."

"Battle ready?"

"Yes. Your job is to help these two foes become friends again.

Here comes one now," he observed, looking to his right. "And here comes the other," looking to his left.

I followed his gaze, and I saw two girls approaching us up the street from both directions. Neither one would look at the other, but both looked at Professor Skye and me.

"Pull up some curb," invited Professor Skye, and one girl, the taller, sat beside him, while the shorter one sat by me.

"This is Mr. Rory McCrory," Professor Skye announced, meaning me. Then, reversing the introductions: "And this is Binney" (the tall girl) "and Sara" (the short one). Neither girl looked pleased to meet me.

"I'm glad I don't have a name as funny as that," said Binney and made a sour face. "I'd get teased worse than I already am. 'Skinny Binney' is bad enough."

"Well, it's not my fault!" answered Sara.

"Is too!"

"Is not!"

"Is too! When they gang up on me on the playground, you join right in. Some friend you are! Nice when we're alone, and mean when we're at school."

"I wasn't joining in. I wasn't saying anything."

"That's the same as joining in. If we're best friends, how come you didn't stand up for me?"

"And get teased, too? Why should I? I suppose then you'd stand up for me?"

"I would!"

"Would not!"

"Would too!"

"This is why," interrupted Professor Skye, "Mr. Rory McCrory is with us. He settles arguments."

I did? I did not! But Professor Skye just smiled and leaned back, while the two girls both looked to me for help.

"Arguments," I began, having absolutely no idea of what I was about to say, "arguments are about who is right and who is wrong."

"So what?" said Sara, who was quieter than Binney but, it seemed to me, was the more confident of the two.

"Some help you are!" snapped Binney.

73

Maybe I needed to begin again.

"How long have you been best friends?" I asked Binney.

"Forever," she answered. "I guess not anymore."

"Why not?"

"Ask her. She'd rather be popular than be my friend."

"Is that true?" I asked Sara.

"No. Not really. She's just jealous because now I'm in with the social crowd."

"The Snob Squad, you mean," corrected Binney. "Nice to each other, but mean to everybody else. Stuck on themselves. Now you'll think you're too good for me!"

"Will not!"

"Will too!"

"Will not!"

"You already do. Treating me like I'm contagious and you better stay away. Or you might catch it."

"Catch what?" I asked.

"I don't know," Binney answered. "Maybe unpopularity. If she hangs out with them, then she can't hang out with me. At least not at school. Isn't that right?"

I could see Sara didn't want to answer, so I just waited. At last she did.

"It's not like we're married, Binney! I can make other friends if I want to."

"Not like me, you can't."

"I didn't say like you.'

"No, but that's what you meant."

"Did not!"

"Did too!"

"Did not!"

This wasn't getting us anywhere, I thought, so I said so.

"I don't see how who wins the argument is going to help the friendship. What good will blaming do? Is anger all you feel? Don't you feel anything else?"

Neither one spoke and I didn't either. All four of us sat without saying a word. Professor Skye, the most silent of all, nodded like he understood.

"I feel sad." It was Sara speaking.

"She's not the only one who misses how we were." It was Binney.

"How were you?" I asked.

"Always talking. We'd talk for hours on the phone at night. Not anymore. She won't call me and I won't call her. We're both too mad."

This reminded me of my sister. Determined to stay angry no matter how much it hurt.

Then I thought I saw a way.

"Maybe you can talk about what you miss instead of what you're mad at," I suggested. "That way no one has to win, and there isn't any right or wrong."

More silence.

"I guess we could try." This time it was Binney who spoke first.

"Thank you, Mr. McCrory," announced Professor Skye, as though it was time to get on to whatever came next.

"There isn't much I can add to what each of you has said," he looked at them both, "except this: One of the hardest hurts in growing up is when best friends begin to grow apart. The most important thing is to remember that it isn't anybody's fault. One person can feel selfish for wanting to move on, while the other may feel lonely from being left behind. What Mr. McCrory said is true. It's something to be more sad about than angry."

And both girls looked sad when Professor Skye said this. Then Binney brightened up.

"Do you want to come over?' she asked.

"Sure," Sara replied. "We can stop at the store on the way for a snack. I've got some money."

Both got up.

"You're all right for a boy with such a funny name," said Binney to me.

"Yeah, thanks," agreed Sara.

Then they walked off together, while I watched and wondered.

"Your question is," interrupted Professor Skye, "Why would Sara want new friends when she is best friends with Binney?"

"Well, why would she?" I asked.

"Because as people grow and change, their desire for friendship changes, too. But it sure can hurt when the person you like the most starts liking someone else."

I thought about Mom and my sister. How they had grown much closer after the divorce, and now Mom was wanting to be friends with Henry. No wonder my sister was so unhappy. First she lost Dad. Now she was losing Mom.

"Well," said Professor Skye. "It's time for me to go. You won't be seeing me again for a while."

I was startled.

"Because you won't be needing me?" I asked, feeling disappointed.

"No. Because *you* won't be needing *me*. From helping others you have learned to help yourself."

"For a long while?" I wanted to know. He wasn't exactly like a friend, but I would miss him. He had become part of my life.

"Now that you mention it, you might see me during our next case. If you look carefully enough."

I heard a familiar rattle and glanced up the street. This was why my sister and I called Mom's car the Clunker. You could hear it coming a mile away. And sure enough, they turned the corner, driving slowly because that was the only way it drove. From their expressions I could tell the meeting at school had not been happy. Mom looked real determined, and my sister wore a frown.

"Did you find anyone?" asked my mom.

"Professor Skye," I answered without thinking, and turned to introduce him to her. But of course he wasn't there.

She shook her head, climbed out of the car, and walked inside the house. My sister stayed in her seat.

"How was it?" I asked.

"Terrible! Mom's ganged up on me. She and the school. I hate the way she's changed!"

"You liked her the old way better," I said, kind of repeating what she had said.

"She doesn't care if I like her or not anymore. She only cares about doing the right thing. That's what she told me in the car. And I am doing better. But it makes me angry!"

"It sounds like you miss how it used to be," I said. "You and Mom having fun together."

My sister nodded.

"You still could, you know. You don't have to stay angry all the time."

Now my sister shook her head. "If I don't stay angry," she confessed, "I'm afraid I'd cry."

"Is that so bad?"

"I don't want her to know. She wouldn't care. All she cares about is Henery!"

"Maybe so." I didn't want to argue. "But you might give it a try. The worst that could happen is that you'd end up where you are: angry all the time."

"Supper!" It was Mom calling. So we went inside.

No one said anything. We ate in silence. Afterward, while we cleaned up the dishes, Mom had one of her long phone talks with Henry.

By the time she got off, we were in our room, reading.

Mom came in and sat down on my sister's bed. At first my sister pretended not to notice and kept reading, but Mom didn't go away. She didn't say anything. She just sat there. And soon my sister lowered her book and put her head on Mom's lap and Mom began to stroke her hair. That's when my sister began to cry. And then to really cry, to sob and sob. Mom just kept stroking her head and rubbing her back. Neither one of them spoke a word. Mom stayed right there for a long time, until I could tell by the heavy breathing that my sister was asleep. Then, very gently, Mom replaced her lap with a pillow, kissed me, and turned out the light.

A couple of times, I woke up that night to hear my sister whimpering in her sleep.

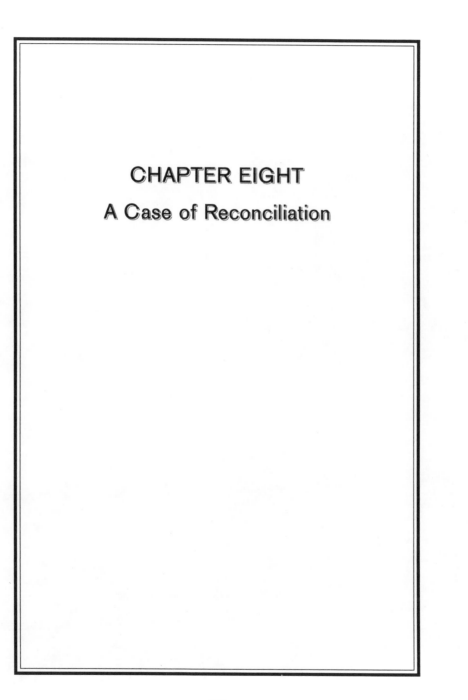

# CHAPTER EIGHT

## A Case of Reconciliation

If I don't ever go through another day like the following Sunday, that will be too soon. Even though things did turn out for the best.

My sister woke up early while Mom and I were still asleep. About an hour later I got up. When I stumbled into the kitchen still feeling groggy, there was my sister sitting on the floor, feeding pieces of cheese to a little brown puppy like the one I had met at Sosa's, except grown bigger.

"Where did the puppy come from?" I asked.

"Isn't he the sweetest thing?" crooned my sister. "He loves me and I love him!" The little dog finished eating and curled up in my sister's lap while she scratched behind his ears.

"Where did you get him?" I repeated.

"You're not going to believe this," she answered, "but it's true. Not made up like your Professor Skye. At about 6:30 I heard someone knocking on the door. And when I opened it, there was a short, gray-haired lady standing on the steps.

" 'You lose a dog?' she asked.

"I said, 'No,' we didn't have a dog.

" 'You so sure?' she asked again.

"That's when this little dog rushed out from behind her and jumped into my arms, licking my face.

" 'Sure act like your dog,' the woman said. 'Why you no have a dog? You no like dogs?'

" 'I love dogs!' I protested.

" 'Good! This one, he belong to you.' Then she turned and walked away leaving the puppy in my arms. Of course, I put him down so he could run after her. But he didn't. He just cried to be held again. Maybe he was hungry, I thought, so I brought him inside. And he was. He drank some milk, ate some leftover chili from last night, and now he's eaten some cheese. A dog? Can you believe it? My very own dog!"

"Mom won't like it," I warned. "You know how she feels about pets. We have enough to take care of without adding any animals."

"I don't care!" my sister stubbornly declared. "I love him and he loves me!"

It was then I knew we were in trouble. And I was right. Because when Mom walked in, her first question was: "What is this puppy doing here?"

So my sister repeated what she had explained to me.

Mom listened, but shook her head in disapproval. She didn't believe the part about the old woman.

"You sound just like your brother, telling stories. But this dog is real enough. We need to find him another home."

"This *is* his home," insisted my sister.

"No it's not! I've told you both before: no pets! We can't afford the time or the expense. The puppy goes!"

"If he does," threatened my sister, "then I do, too!"

But I knew Mom better than that. Once she took a stand, she didn't back down.

"How do you want to go about finding him a home?" Mom asked.

"I don't and I won't! It's just not fair! Dad has Marie. You have Henery. Even my brother has his Professor Skye. But who do I have? No one! I can't even have a dog!" And crying in anger, she picked up the puppy and bolted out the kitchen door.

"You come back here!" ordered Mom.

But my sister and the dog were gone.

"She'll come back," my mother told herself.

But I wasn't so sure. I'd never seen my sister so defiant and determined. After an hour, I could see my mother wasn't feeling so sure, either.

"Where can she have gone?" she asked me.

"I don't know. Maybe we ought to go and look for her."

So we did. We searched the neighborhood for another hour, but she was nowhere to be found.

By the time we got home, Mom had her mind made up. She did something I never thought she would. She called my dad and told him all about what had happened. He said he'd be right over, and he was. When she opened the door, he gave her a hug and she hugged him back. It felt strange seeing them together.

"We'd better call the police," Dad said, and then saw a patrol car cruising slowly down the street. He rushed outside to flag it down. Out of the car stepped Officer LaSalle. But when he followed Dad inside, he showed no sign of recognizing me.

"Our daughter's run away," Mom began, and told about the puppy and the argument before my sister left.

"Running away is when she has some place she wants to go," replied Officer LaSalle after hearing Mom out. "This here is just running off. She won't go far. We'll find her," he promised, and his confidence calmed my mother down. "You stay here by the phone in case someone calls." Then turning to my dad: "You and your boy come along with me."

I'd never ridden in a police car before. Dad sat beside Officer LaSalle while I sat in the back behind a shotgun that was locked between the two front seats. He talked to my dad as we rode.

"Shouldn't be too hard to track her down, young girl carrying a little dog. These days lots of kids running the streets. Families splitting up. Moms can't do it all. Kids can get lost without their fathers. Boys left to learn how to be men from other boys. Girls learning from boys what men are like. Kids teaching kids because their parents ain't around. We'll try the park." And he swung the car into a slow circle around the big playground, stopping near a young boy, calling him over.

"A girl holding a dog come through here?"

It was Sonny McWalter, but without the flashlight.

"A brown puppy? Yeah. A while ago. She was in a hurry. Crossed over by the swimming pool and headed down Tooney Boulevard."

"Thanks." And we drove in the same direction.

"Not a lot of people out on Sunday morning." Officer LaSalle pulled to a sudden stop, as a small girl speeding on a bicycle veered to avoid us.

"Your parents know you ride like this?" he asked.

She looked away and mumbled something.

"Say what?" he asked.

"Yes," she said. "No," she admitted.

"Jessalyn, what did I tell you about crossing streets?"

"To wait for a break in the traffic before I do, and cross at the corners."

"So?"

"Next time I will. I promise. That's the truth."

"It better be. You see a girl holding a dog?"

"I saw a girl holding a puppy. She was walking slow. Maybe lost. She stopped to look into the grocery store window and then turned the corner toward the high school."

"One thing about running off," said Officer LaSalle, waving good-bye to Jessalyn, "sooner or later you get tired. No planning, so usually no money and no food."

The high school was deserted except for two girls sitting on the steps. They were talking so intensely they didn't notice us drive up. Two best friends for a while longer.

"Hey!" called Officer LaSalle. "Come here."

The taller girl looked up.

"Us?"

Officer LaSalle nodded.

They walked slowly over, like they were going to be accused of doing something wrong.

"Information is all. I'm looking for a girl carrying a little dog. You see her?"

"Sure," replied the shorter girl, brightening up. "She let us pet him. He was cute. Something wrong?"

"Just need to find her. Notice where she went?"

"We gave her directions," said the taller one. "She wanted a place where she could use a phone. The church on Forsythe was just letting out. We sent her there." He nodded thanks, and they walked away.

Wait a minute! Something was going on was how I felt. Like Professor Skye had told me, it was foolish to believe in accidents. This was just too much coincidence: the old lady, the puppy, Officer LaSalle, Sonny McWalter, Jessalyn, and now Sara and Binney.

84

They were all playing a part in some plan Professor Skye had put together. But what? I didn't know, but now I didn't have to worry, either. With Professor Skye in charge, I felt my sister would be taken care of, would be all right.

"Trail's getting warmer," said Officer LaSalle. "Won't be long before we're running up on her."

My dad had been very quiet so far, into himself, not saying much. Thinking.

"I'll blame myself if she gets hurt," he spoke at last.

"Here's the church," said Officer LaSalle, not replying. Letting my dad listen to his own words. "Doors are closed. Morning service must be over. We'll try out back." And he drove around behind.

There were a few parked cars and a couple of kids shooting baskets on a half court painted on the corner of the lot. They were playing one on one, the smaller boy taking it to the larger, who didn't make it easy but kept from being rough. I recognized Eldridge and Lamar, who recognized Officer LaSalle.

"What's happening?" he asked, climbing out of the car.

Lamar threw him the ball, and officer LaSalle lofted a long three pointer that swished the net.

"No flies on me!"

"Pretty sharp," smiled Lamar.

"You men seen a girl come through holding a dog?"

"Maybe a quarter ago," answered Lamar. "Walking home with a family, talking to the mom. I think they live about two blocks down, on Jefferson off Dennis."

"I know the place. Young brother's going to take you one of these days." Officer LaSalle got back into the car.

"Maybe," laughed Lamar. "But if he does, it's 'cause I taught him how." And they went back to their game.

"You let me know when you spot your daughter."

Dad nodded and looked out the window at the houses and apartments as we passed.

"There!" he shouted, and jumped out as we were slowing down. I waited until we had stopped before I followed.

On the steps of a house sat my sister, the puppy in her lap, both looking pretty tired, next to a tall woman who glanced up as soon as she saw my father. Regina Lee's mother, and she wasn't smiling.

"You belong to this girl?"

My dad nodded, pausing awkwardly like he wasn't sure what to do.

"Where you been? You think a daughter doesn't need her father? That's what she believes. I told her she was wrong. Without you there, she's going to get a lot of no good men in her life. You want that?"

My dad shook his head.

"Then she better spend some time with you and you with her. Hear?" Then to my sister: "You hear what I'm saying, Girl?"

My sister got to her feet, the puppy in her arms. One step toward my dad was all it took before he swept her up, puppy and all, squeezing her tight.

"Time to get home," called Officer LaSalle. And then to me: "Your mom's had a trial of waiting."

Now I was in the front seat while Dad and my sister sat close together in the back.

I don't know why, but something made me look over my shoulder as we drove off, and I caught a glimpse of Regina Lee's mother standing on her porch talking to a man who looked familiar. He turned toward me and waved, and I waved back. Then each of us was out of the other's sight.

"See someone you know?" asked my father.

"In a way," I answered. "In a way." And I was silent, thinking, for the rest of the drive home. Thinking about Professor Skye.

"Thanks, Officer," said Dad as we pulled up.

"No problem," replied Officer LaSalle. "Just take care of your kids."

"I will," promised my dad, getting out. "I will."

Mom stood on the curb waiting for my sister, who wasn't ready to get out. At least, not yet.

"Do I get to keep the puppy?" she asked. Not a threat. Just a question.

Mom looked at Dad and nodded her head.

"I can't be right about everything," she said. "And this time I was wrong. The puppy stays. All of us need someone."

Just then the phone rang, and I ran inside to answer it.

"It's Henery!" I yelled from the front door.

"Henry," corrected Mom as she came inside.

Dad and my sister walked up behind.

"Would you like to come and visit next weekend?" asked Dad. "You can bring the puppy."

My sister nodded.

"I'll ask your mom if I can pick you up."

And after she got off the phone with Henry, Mom agreed.

Dad hung around a little while to call Marie and let her know my sister was okay. As he was leaving, Mom stopped him at the door.

"Thanks," she said.

He sighed like he felt relieved.

"Thank you," he replied. And squeezed her hand good-bye.

That night in bed I told Mom it was good to see her and Dad being okay together after all this time, and she said it felt good to her.

"I'm even feeling glad you like Marie."

"Truly?" I asked.

"Yes, some good has to come from all these changes, and that includes Marie. I think your dad just got scared about growing old. I couldn't give him what he needed, but I think Marie can. Now I'm ready to get on with my life, too. Who knows, maybe someone's out there waiting for me. We'll just have to see."

Then she kissed me and my sister good night, and the puppy, who was curled up on my sister's bed. Turning out the lights, she closed the door.

"I want to ask you something," whispered my sister.

"Sure," I replied.

"What shall I name the puppy?"

"Whatever you want," I answered.

"I want you to name him."

"Me?" The name came right away. "Sosa," I said. "Call him Sosa."

"'Sosa.' I like it," my sister said. "How did you think of a name like that?"

"Just my imagination," I explained. "You know how I like to make things up. Good night."

And that's the last I saw of Professor Skye. For a while. But I've written down each case like you said I should. As best I remember. Stories no one would believe but you, Marie, so you became the only one I told.

## THE END

(until the next time)